"Sally Wright doesn't create characters—she breeds living, breathing people right there on the page. Along with her meticulously researched and developed background and intricate plot, *The Outsiding* is a practically perfect book. And her historical notes at the end are almost as interesting as the novel itself."

—Donna Fletcher Crow, Award-winning author of *Glastonbury*; Lord Danvers Investigates; The Monastery Murders; and the Elizabeth and Richard Literary Suspense.

"With her characteristic mastery of words, Sally Wright engages her reader with the last of her Jo Grant mystery series, located deep in the heart of horse country, Lexington, Kentucky. Set in the 1960's, the thoroughbred breeding industry is undermined by a cunning and highly disreputable veterinarian's ingenious money-making schemes. The reader is treated to a skillfully woven plot and a cleverly constructed cast of characters who lead us into the darker side of the horse racing and breeding world as well as into the inevitable pitfalls of family business and interpersonal interactions. A mystery sure to absorb horse enthusiasts as well as those who savor this popular author's mastery of words and intrigue. Saddle up for a captivating read."

—Peggy S. Brown, Equestrian instructor and clinician

"Bad blood across the generations is brought to a boil with the discovery of a long-hidden murder weapon and a wealth of silver, the least of Jo Grant Munro's problems in *The Outsiding*. With a sure hand Wright sets the scene in Kentucky's horse breeding country, populating a superb mystery with characters as sharp as the snap of a horse whip. And Sally Wright handles the notion of her main character with a clever aplomb. A rewarding read!"

—Jim Benn, *Solemn Graves*

Praise for *Behind the Bonehouse*, Jo Grant Mystery 2

"With elegant prose and graceful storytelling, Sally Wright delivers another compelling novel set in the beautiful horse country of Kentucky. Although there's plenty of mystery afoot, family is at the heart of this tale [as she] intricately weaves together the lives of her characters and the land they call home."

—William Kent Krueger, NY Times Best Selling, Edgar Award winning author of the Cork O'Connor Mystery Series.

"Wright gives us a story of Kentucky horse country that's articulate and frighteningly possible, a setting that is pitch perfect, and characters who step right off the page; a bittersweet look at people you care about and want to win, a novel you won't soon forget."

—Charles Todd, bestselling author of the Inspector Ian Rutledge Mysteries and the Bess Crawford Series

THE OUTSIDING

by

Sally Wright

Print Edition ISBN: 978-0-9827801-5-2

Print layout by booknook.biz

To Joey
and Dylan
and Vivien,
in order of appearance.

With many thanks too
to Rod Morris,
my long-time editor.

LIST OF CHARACTERS

Cook, Glenn — equine painter

Fisher, Mick — groom Michael meets at Bud's

Fletcher, Sara — Office Manager, MacInnes Equine

Franklin, Spencer — friend of Jo's, with cousins in Middleburg

Freemantle, Isaiah — 1800s owner of Glenn's house

Freemantle, Marcella — Samuel Freemantle's cousin, Ronnie Holmes's aunt

Freemantle, Samuel — former owner of Glenn's house

Harris, Dutton — veterinarian managing MacInnes Equine

Harris, Elizabeth — Dutton's mother

Harris, Willard — Dutton's deceased father

Holmes, Ronnie — Michael's friend, employed at MacInnes Equine

Jones, Buddy — Jo's friend, an assistant horse trainer

Judd, Barclay — owner of Midway Farm

Kreuzer, Annabelle — woman murdered in Glenn's house

Kreuzer, Matilda — Annabelle's daughter

Kreuzer, Randall — Annabelle's speech impaired son

MacInnes, Alex — Michael MacInnes' son

MacInnes, Clifford — Michael MacInnes' father, Meg's deceased husband

MacInnes, Margaret (Meg) — owner of MacInnes Equine Vet Services, Cliff's widow, Michael's mother

MacInnes, Missy — Meg's deceased daughter

Madden, Anna — widow of Phillip Madden

Madden, Phillip — deceased Louisville vet

Metzger, Rhoda — horse owner, client of MacInnes Equine

Metzger, Wesley — husband of Rhoda, client of MacInnes Equine

Miller, Carl — client of MacInnes Equine

Miller, Susie — daughter of Carl, owner of Whiskers

Munro, Alan — Jo's husband, chemical engineer at Equine Pharmaceuticals

Munro, Jo Grant — architect, Meg's friend and landlady

Munro, Ross — Jo and Alan's toddler son

Peabody, Earl — Woodford County Sheriff

Prince, Eliza — works in reception at MacInnes Equine

Petrosky, Nancy — employee at MacInnes Equine

Petrosky, Marie — Nancy's brain damaged sister

Rattigan, Dave — farm manager at Midway farm

Reynolds, Dr. William — doctor at St. Joseph's Hospital

Rineholt, Jerry — vet at MacInnes Equine Vet Services

Russell, Ridgeway — lawyer and friend of the MacInneses

Smalls, Charlie — stallion groom at Claiborne Farm

Smalls, Tate — stallion groom, cousin of Charlie Smalls and Esther Wilkes

Snyder, Harry — owner of Aldernay Farm

Sperry, Frank — retired breeding manager, friend of the MacInneses

Stevens, Laura — Michael's fiancée

Swede, Mort — barn manager at Aldernay Farm

Swede, Webber — half-brother of Mort, works at MacInnes Equine

Watkins, Toss — Jo Grant Munro's uncle who runs their broodmare care business

Wilkes, Esther — cousin of Tate Smalls, twin sister of Charlie Smalls

THE GATE

A month or two before I finished writing *Behind The Bonehouse*, the son of a woman I knew well years ago called and asked if he could see me. His mother had died fifteen years earlier at the age of ninety-one, having become something like a mother to me when she was in her seventies and I was in my early thirties. He and I hadn't been in touch much in the last year, and I was surprised by the urgency in his voice—so much that I postponed a meeting with a client, whose farmhouse I was renovating, so Michael could drive straight over.

He came in fast, tall and thin still, but older looking than when I'd seen him last, and handed me an envelope addressed to me in his mother's hand along with a box of reel-to-reel tapes. "I found the letter this morning in the back of a drawer in my desk. After she died, I packed up her office, and brought it all home, and sorted through everything gradually over the next few months.

"I don't know how your letter got shoved in my

desk drawer, but it did, with another letter for me that I only found today asking me to give you these tapes. I should've paid attention, and read the letter, and gotten it all to you then."

I said, "She'd just died. And with the funeral arrangements—"

"Our son was in that car accident then too, and there were months there where… well, you remember what that was like. But I owe you an apology. There's no excuse for it taking this long."

Michael and I talked about our families then, and his work and mine, and Alan's too, and how my health is at the moment, and then he hugged me and said we should get together for dinner soon.

I watched him drive out the front circle into the long front lane, and then I sat at the desk in my office and opened the letter. Once I began to read it, I could hear Meg talking to me just the way she had when I was young.

December 7, 1975
Dear Jo,

I have left Michael two sets of tapes I recorded as a diary with the intention that he give one to you. You have nearly become a daughter to me, as you know very well. And I want you to have them as a reminder of the years when I lived in your cabin, and our lives were so entwined—with our walks, and our dogs, and our care for each other.

I do, however, have an ulterior motive, which I shall reveal shortly.

I recorded the tapes in much the way you used your journal to understand and accept what you and Alan went through years ago. Using a microphone comes more easily to me than typing or writing my thoughts in longhand, and it enables me to speak more naturally and move more swiftly as well, having often recorded my piano work when tackling a difficult passage.

It would be a kindness if you would listen to the tapes. Circumstances you know well led me to use the recordings as a record of what we'd feared, from one day to the next, then found we faced, as the clinic was ripped away from us.

And here, my dear, is the crux of the matter, for if you are willing, I very much hope you will write an account for Michael's children, and whatever offspring they may have, of what you will find on these tapes—the chronological uncovering of the systematic wickedness that tore Cliff's life work asunder, and nearly took two lives.

If, however, you decide a useful purpose would be served, I would certainly be willing for the account to be written for publication, especially because of the attempts by the guilty party and his family to deflect all blame since the facts came to light. You're my favorite teller of anecdotes, and I believe you may be a writer, Jo. I believe the traits that have made you an architect also account for you being as observant as you are with people, and having a facility with words as well.

You've been such a blessing to me. You, and Alan, and the boys too. And I look forward to meeting you in a better world.

Meg

After I listened to Meg's tapes, I knew this was a book I had to write. It would've been easier for me fifteen years ago, when I didn't have the health troubles I have now, but I can't not set about it, for I believe it's work I'm meant to do.

Since Michael brought me the tapes, I have interviewed him at length, and the handful of others who'd been more directly involved than I was at the time, which has forced me to learn more about equine medicine than I ever expected I could.

I have also used excerpts from my own journals to give the day-to-day immediacy of what it felt like back then, while I told the story of what actually happened as though it were a novel, slipping myself in, like any other character, looking back from the outside, the way I did in *Breeding Ground* and *Behind The Bonehouse*.

I'm sixty-eight now, still younger than Meg was when she went through these events, but I know more now, having lived this long, about what the strain must've been for her, with my own children grown up, making their way as well.

I hope good will come from making this public—that those who read what Meg experienced will learn what will help them face their own reversals, now, or in the future.

Jo Grant Munro
December 1998
Rolling Ridge Farm
McCowan's Ferry Road
Versailles, Kentucky

CHAPTER ONE

Wednesday, February 17, 1965

Meg MacInnes had to sell the house. She'd seen that when her husband, Cliff, died a little more than a year before. It was an 1810 Kentucky brick farmhouse, and it was too large and too costly to run, and she couldn't take care of it by herself. When a big Irish stud farm bought up the land around her, she'd decided to accept their offer and rent an old cabin on a friend's farm that was in the process of being restored and added-on to.

She was gradually giving away clothes and books and years of accumulated household goods she didn't need at this stage in her life that someone else could use. She'd put three bags of clothes in the backseat of her Dodge, and four boxes of books in the trunk, and had just come in to grab her pocketbook, when she heard a car in the drive.

It was a long drive up a fairly high hill with a gravel circle by the front porch, and she watched an old gray

Chevy pull up—the paint dull, the fenders rusting, the face behind the wheel one she knew well.

Nancy Petrosky. One of those souls who suffer unaccountably seemingly from birth.

She'd worked for Cliff at MacInnes Equine Veterinary Services for almost twenty years and was probably close to forty-five now, though she'd always looked older than she was. Her watery brown eyes seemed too big for their sockets, and they aimed off in opposite directions making it hard to know where to look when you were trying to converse. Her hair was limp and mole-colored, and her face was broad and puffy with an oddly contoured nose and a small mouth that seemed to disappear beneath her wandering eyes—which had to have made her childhood a nightmare of mockery and abuse.

Meg had heard Nancy described by a long-gone employee as "a pudding of a person"—and she *was* short and somewhat shapeless, and she did wear clothes that made her look like she'd come from some Eastern bloc country.

But she was willing to do anything at the clinic, and she had a great respect for learning, as well as a natural ability to work with horses who were afraid or in pain. Cliff had trained her to assist him in several clinical procedures and to take meticulous medical histories too when she helped register patients. She disinfected the operating room and sterilized the equipment. And once a month she deep cleaned the lab, the offices, and the supply rooms to make extra money.

The burden she rarely talked about, but carried every

day of her life, was that when her parents had died ten years earlier they'd left the care of her brain-damaged sister entirely in her hands. She'd sworn Marie would never go into an institution, and her every waking minute revolved around keeping her safe.

Even so, at that moment the thought uppermost in Meg's mind was, *Why isn't Nancy at work?*

Meg stepped through the door as Nancy climbed the stairs, seeing that second that something was really wrong, before she said, "Hey, honey. It's good to see you. How 'bout a cup of coffee?"

"No, thank you. I can see you were fixin' to leave. If we could just sit here on the porch for a minute that'd be fine with me."

"Whatever you want to do."

They both sat on old teak garden chairs—the breeze gentle and the sun helping to warm the morning—Nancy looking self-conscious and distressed, Meg smoothing her blue wool skirt, pulling her jacket closer around her, waiting for Nancy to settle herself and say what she wanted to say.

"Dr. Harris let me go."

"What!" Meg sat up straight and stared hard at Nancy, concentrating finally on Nancy's right eye.

"Yes, ma'am, he did. And I thought maybe with all the folks you know who're veterinarians around town, you might could tell me who I should talk to, and maybe even—"

"I'll give you an excellent recommendation. And do anything else I can think of to help. But I'm having trouble understanding this. Why did he say he's letting you go?"

"I don't come up to his standards, I guess. He said he wants folks with more education, and I'd have to go to make way. Dr. Cliff used to make me feel like I did pretty good at my work, and he was such a fine man to work for, I—"

"He thought you did your work extremely well! He said you were an asset to the clinic and a great help to him. How much notice did Dr. Harris give you?"

"He paid me for two weeks, but told me not to come back. I didn't even get to say goodbye to folks." Nancy's plump face was pink now.

And Meg could see she was trying hard to keep herself from crying. "Sit right there. I'll be back in a minute."

Meg came back with her checkbook and began to write out a check.

"I can't let you do that! No, ma'am, I didn't intend for you to—"

"I'm going to, so you better make up your mind to it. And I'll do it again if it takes you a while to find a new place. What are you doing with Marie these days?"

"Well, when I'm home, I keep all the doors locked way up high on the inside so she can't get out and wander off, even if she gets up and walks in the night."

"Remind me how old she is." Meg pushed a long gray hairpin farther into her chignon, and then eased the check from the pad.

"She's thirty-two and she's real strong, and when she

takes a notion to do something, it can be kinda hard to make her give it up. Mentally she's a little child. Somethin' like three or four."

"It's been a while since we talked about her, and I couldn't quite remember. What do you do when you're at work?"

"I take her to a kinda elderly lady who was a friend of my mama's and she watches her at her house. I pay her as much as I can, but she's getting on in years, and with Marie getting harder to handle, I don't know what…" Nancy stopped then and swallowed and seemed to look past both their cars toward the edge of the hill. "This morning, when I was takin' a shower, Marie went out to the garage. I don't lock that door every minute so she's got some place to run around inside.

"I got a cabinet there where I lock things up I don't want Marie to get into, like the toilet paper and the cleaning supplies and peanut butter too, 'cause she won't stop eating it once she starts. I forgot to set the combination lock last night, and she got in and took out six rolls of toilet paper and strung it all over in the garage and the house. It was my fault, I know that, but I was countin' on that toilet paper to last another week. It took me an hour to get just some little part of it cleaned up 'cause a bunch of things broke when she wrapped the paper around stuff. I don't know what to say about it, 'cept it was kinda like the last straw." Tears had started down Nancy's cheeks, and she swallowed hard, and it almost sounded as though she'd gagged as she tried to make herself stop.

"I'm so sorry." Meg leaned over and patted Nancy's shoulder, then handed her a check for what she would've gotten paid for a month at MacInnes. "I'll bring the letters of recommendation over to you tonight. And I'll phone the vets I know around town, and see who else I can think of to talk to."

"You don't have to—"

"You were a real help to Cliff. You were, with the surgeries and the medical histories. He relied on you to do everything well. And it's not right. I know it's not. And I wish I could turn it around, but I can't. Even though I still own the practice, Harris is in charge now, and it'd be a mistake for me to go in after the fact and try to force him to change a decision, even though I'd like to."

Nancy nodded and pulled a handkerchief out of the pocket of her sagging sweater, then dabbed at her eyes before she stood.

Meg got up and wrapped her arms around her, leaning down a little to lay the side of her face against Nancy's. "I don't know how this will work out, but it will. We're not going to give up. We'll find you a job that's something you like, and look for help with Marie too."

"Jo, there's something you should see." Glenn Cook had limped through the doorway from his half-finished bedroom into what would end up being his library-dining room when the carpentry was done, the second he heard Jo step through the front door.

"Where? In the bedroom?" She walked through the wide archway from the front hall, tall and thin and dark haired, and set her roll of blueprints on the dining room mantel on her way toward Glenn.

"We found it when we were taking out the wall between the old sitting room and the small bedroom." Glenn adjusted the metal knee joint on the brace on top of his left pant leg, then pivoted back through the doorway.

Half the stud wall was missing now, to the left of the gaping opening where the old French doors had been taken down, but Glenn was focusing his Nikon camera on a shattered space on the right side of that archway where a two-foot patch of plaster and lath had just been hammered away.

"Look inside the wall on the floor. There was already a piece of lath missing there when Ray opened it up."

"That's odd."

"Wait till you see the rest."

"Where is Ray, anyway? I thought he was working here all day."

"He went to pick up the bathroom tile after we found this. Look."

There was still a strip of plaster under the hole at the bottom, maybe a foot or so high, and when Jo looked behind it, down to where the wall met the floor, she saw what looked like a crumpled cloth bag, and a jumble of handleless cups and silverware, covered now with plaster and an older layer of dust.

"I'm going to photograph everything just the way we found it before we take it out."

"So the Freemantles can't accuse you of stealing anything that's here."

"Exactly."

"It must be theirs. They built the house in the 1850s, and put the wall in twenty years later, and they've owned it ever since."

"I bet I know who'll want it." Glenn grinned.

And Jo laughed. "Requiring no great insight on your part. Have you ever heard where the old woman was shot?"

"Here in her sitting room. At least according to the real estate agent."

Jo had shaken out her thick dark hair and was putting it back up in a ponytail as she watched Glenn photograph the whole inside of the wall.

They glanced at each other for half a second as though they were both making sure they were ready, and then Glenn reached into the hole and pulled out the cloth sack, and laid it, with four blackened cups and a handful of tarnished utensils, onto a sheet of plywood sitting on two sawhorses by the front wall.

Jo bent over the tarnished cups, which were narrower at the bottom than the top, and blew off a small cloud of dust. "They're julep cups. Old ones. One of them's engraved too. 'Ky. State… Agr. Society… 1856.' It's probably solid silver. And the other three must be earlier.

They've got the silversmith Asa Blanchard's mark, so they must be worth a good deal of money. Whatever's in the bag is heavy."

There was a string tie keeping the bag closed, and as Glenn worked to undo the knot, plaster dust billowing all around them, the string broke and the cloth ripped apart and an old handgun, and a handful of jewelry, and several sheets of stiff speckled paper fell onto the plywood.

They both stood and stared. And then, as Jo reached for the papers, Glenn said, "Wait a minute. Let me document everything first."

He did. Quickly, expertly, a professional painter who used a camera every day, photographing the group together—his light-brown hair falling on his forehead as he leaned over the table.

"Why would anyone have put these things in the wall?"

Glenn didn't answer. He was thinking about focal lengths and varying exposures—till he wiped his forehead with a handkerchief that turned black with dust and dirt, his hazel eyes looking at Jo as though he could see her mind. "You ready to read me the papers while I shoot every piece by itself?"

"I thought you'd never ask!" Jo's straight dark eyebrows were tucked down and concentrating, half-hiding her dark-blue eyes, as she picked up the yellowed pages and wiped them with his handkerchief.

She walked to the front window and turned the papers to the light, having to work to pry them open against the crinkled folds.

The 23rd day of July in the year 1874

I, Matilda Louise Kreuzer, am writing this... document of my own free will. I, with no assistance or collusion, shot and killed my mother, Annabelle Freemantle Kreuzer, on this night... a trifle after ten o'clock, using a .22 caliber revolver, previously owned by my father, William Wesley Kreuzer. I take full and complete responsibility for my actions, which occurred without premeditation.

Jo shook her head as she read, and then looked over at Glenn. "The ink's really faded, and it's nineteenth century script, which I'm not great at, and I'll give you an extract when I have to."

"Good." Glenn was focusing on the jewelry—two pairs of earrings, one broach, a jet necklace, and two Intaglio onyx rings—listening while he worked.

My mother has long spoken to my brother, Randall Elijah Kreuzer, who was born with a misshapen mouth and is unable to speak properly, in the most unkind and belittling of terms, repeatedly referring to his unfortunate deficiencies with such... contempt that I have developed a deep-seated and remorseless resentment of her ceaseless cruelty. Once my beloved father passed away, and we came to live under Uncle Isaiah's... protection her criticism and disregard for Randall and myself became nearly unendurable, whether because of her grief, or because of her... frustration at the loss of her own house by fire, I do not know.

Though I became affianced to a young man most congenial to myself, she has inflicted upon my intended such vituperative and scathing remarks I had to end the engagement for his sake, and for mine, and because I was afraid to leave my brother at my mother's mercy.

This evening, after Uncle Isaiah and his groom had left for Lexington with his stallion... Ides of March, intending to compete in a race meeting tomorrow in that city, my mother's remarks to Randall were such that he... fled the house and resorted to the woods beyond the back pasture. Our servants, Mariah and Ezra, have repaired to their own abode, leaving my mother and myself alone in the house.

I cannot adequately describe the state of my mind at that time. Only years of festering anger can begin to account for the... overpowering strength of my rage. I repaired to my bedchamber, and retrieved my father's... pocket revolver from my armoire *and quietly approached my mother in her sitting room, which Uncle Isaiah has kindly partitioned from the former parlor in order to afford my mother a bedroom and an entertaining room for her pleasure.*

The dividing wall was plastered only this morning, and a fire had been lit in the fireplace to assist in drying the plaster. I approached my mother where she sat in her rocking chair at work on her embroidery, and informed her that her viciousness has become unbearable and that Randall had suffered from her mockery for the last time. I stood at her feet and fired at her heart, and watched her die before my eyes...

"*Then* she says she pulled her mother's earrings from her ears… Yikes! … And gathered together other pieces of her jewelry, along with silver presentation cups and other sterling silver belonging to her Uncle Isaiah. And then it looks like she says she scraped away a section of wet plaster from the new wall, and cut away a chunk of lath. She says she'd been interested in how the plasterers had done the wall that morning, and they'd explained their technique and allowed her to plaster a small section.

"So now she says she'll put the jewelry and the silver, with the empty pistol and this confession, inside the wall. That they've left a bucket of wet plaster, to use the next day, and she'll re-plaster and keep the fire lit to help dry the wall."

I shall say I went early to bed with a severe head-ache and was awakened by a shot. Fearing for my life, I came downstairs bearing a heavy… candlestick with which to defend myself, only to hear hoofbeats galloping down the lane, assuming, because of what is missing, that the murderer was a thief who gained entry to the house through the rear door. Rarely do we lock our doors, for we have lived with a sense of safety here, even when Uncle Isaiah is away. And this night, as well, Randall required access…

"Listen to this…"

I do not regret slaying my mother. Yet, I do fear for my immortal soul. I know I cannot pray for forgiveness for I do not feel contrition for silencing her malicious tongue.

May the Lord God lead me to view what I have done as He would have me before it comes my day, as well, to look upon His visage.

Matilda Louise Kreuzer

Neither of them said anything for more than a minute. They gazed at each other, looking stunned and startled, till they heard the front door swing open, and Meg MacInnes's sturdy heels clunk across the heart-pine floor.

She called out, "Jo? Glenn?" in her low, rich, easy-going voice before they called to her to come into the bedroom.

She was just wrapping a wisp of silver hair back toward her chignon—when she saw the mass of antique artifacts set out on the plywood.

Meg said, "Well! This is guaranteed to stir up a hornet's nest. You know Samuel Freemantle—"

"Only too well. He made buying this house as diffi-cult as he could." Glenn handed Meg a filigreed silver earring.

And she studied it before she spoke. "But I don't believe you know the rest of the family."

"No."

"Marcella Freemantle, Jo, you remember she used to work in Dr. Sander's office, and how she could be unpleasant the moment you said, 'Hello'? Not every time, certainly, but—"

"Yes, I definitely do."

"Well, as I'm sure he's told you, Sam's the great-grandson of Isaiah Freemantle who originally owned the house. It was Isaiah's sister who was murdered after he took her and her children in. Now, Isaiah's side always figured it was their ne'er-do-well cousin, Wilfred, who shot Annabelle. He never did a lick a work, he was deep in debt, and running around saying that pretty soon now, he'd have some real money, because then, at that time, Isaiah hadn't married, and had no descendants, and since Annabelle's will excluded the son with the speech impediment, and the daughter as well, *whoever* died first— Isaiah or Annabelle—the cousin, Wilfred, he figured he'd inherit when the last one passed away."

Jo said, "Sounds like a great guy."

"Yes, quite the little opportunist. It was nearly unheard of at the time, but Isaiah went and hired a private investigator from Covington to investigate the murder, and Wilfred came up as the likely suspect, but the grand jury didn't indict him for lack of evidence. And *then,* you see, Isaiah married and had a son, and cousin Wilfred never inherited, and the hard feelings come down till today."

Jo asked if there was anyone left besides Sam and Marcella.

"Ronnie Holmes is Marcella's nephew, another descendent of the scallywag cousin, and some sort of cousin to Sam, but I know he has no interest in perpetuating a feud."

"How do I know the name?" Jo was wiping off a yellow gold mourning broach with a curl of brown hair inside the glass in back.

"He works with Michael at MacInnes Equine. He went to grade school with him too. Ronnie's a very fine person, and he's never had one word to say about the whole thing. But Marcella's as prickly as Samuel, and they surely detest each other."

Glenn said, "Michael's your son, right? I'm sure Jo knows, but—"

"Yes. He's a newly qualified vet."

Jo asked if she knew what had happened to Matilda, the woman who wrote the confession, and her brother.

"She died three or four years after her mother, prob'ly of pneumonia, and her brother two years or so after she did getting thrown off a horse."

Jo said, "How do you know all this? You're an army brat who grew up everywhere but here."

"Cliff knew. He was from over toward Paris, and his family had known everybody going back generations. And, of course, this is the most famous unsolved Kentucky murder from the 1800s."

Glenn had brought in a satchel he used for painting in the field and had set it down by the silver.

Meg had sat down in a wicker chair Jo had brought her from the kitchen, and she was looking for marks on the silverware, while wiping it off with paper towels. "You want me to tell you what I reckon will happen?"

"You feeling kinda prophetic this morning?" Jo laughed, as she drew the outline of a small silver milk pitcher, then made a note in the notebook Glenn had given her as soon as she'd seen the spread eagle with BLANCHARD underneath it.

"No, but I do study human nature." Meg handed her a silver spoon and picked up another. "Marcella will want the confession publicized all over, since it wasn't her ancestor who did the murder. She'll do everything she can to embarrass Samuel by talking about how her ancestor was wrongly accused and *his* relation was a matricide! Sam will want it kept quiet, since her side'll be vindicated, and Ronnie won't care one way or the other. Though I expect he might want a copy of the confession. He's the kind of person who likes to see a true story getting told."

Glenn had taken three rolls of thirty-six exposures each, and he was pulling the last out of the back of the Nikon. "I'm going to enlarge and enhance every page of the confession, as well as the photos of the artifacts. I'll print a bunch of photographic copies—one for me, to stay here in the house, plus whatever it takes for the Freemantle family, and one copy, as well as the original, to take to my lawyer with the revolver, the silver and the jewelry. Once he's seen it, I figure I'll put it all in a safety deposit box till the owner's determined, and we find out if the sheriff has any interest in looking into this, after he's seen a set of pictures."

Jo said that made good sense.

And Glenn put the last of the silver into the canvas

satchel. "I imagine it all belongs to Sam, if he's Isaiah's direct descendent. Though it'd be great if he'd split it up, just to bring peace in the family."

Meg laughed, and her well-worn face looked twenty years younger as soon as she smiled the wide-open smile that'd made a lot of folks in several generations feel better whenever they saw her. "I hope he does. I do. But I'd be mighty surprised."

"And you usually give everybody the benefit of the doubt!" Jo smiled then, and asked Meg if she'd like a glass of iced tea. "The rest of the appliances aren't in, but the refrigerator is."

"Thanks, honey, but not right now. And I did come for a reason, with Glenn not having a phone yet. The plumber arrived at your cabin this morning and said that the kitchen faucet you picked out has been discontinued and you need to go select something else if I'm going to get to move in by March first."

"I'll do it on my way home. What else is getting done today? They're supposed to start sanding the floors tomorrow."

Jo and her husband, Alan, lived on a broodmare care farm, that she ran with her Uncle Toss, which her parents had bought on a shoestring before the Second World War. There'd been an abandoned cabin on the south end of the property that Jo's folks hadn't had the money, or the time, to renovate, especially since her Dad died just before World War II.

But the summer before, in 1964, when Jo and her husband and their infant son, Ross, had been trying to recover from more than one count of near death and destruction, an old farmer down the road, knowing Jo was an architect, said she could have the cabin on his land free if she'd come and move it out of his way. That had given her a reason to renovate the ruins of the old one, and add on a new section that would create a suitable rental property to help with income on the farm.

Jo and Meg talked for a minute about decisions at the cabin, and what needed to be finished next for Meg to move in in early March. "We still need to work out the pantry and laundry area. We can put the shelves wherever you want, but—" Jo could see Meg wasn't listening (when one of her most endearing traits was the way she normally listened to other folks as though they were the only people in her life). She looked tired suddenly, and she was staring out the front window with worry in her eyes, and Jo said, "Why do I have the feeling you're upset about something?"

Meg turned to her then and smiled again, but there was a restrained and uneasy shadow, even before her smile finally faded away. "Oh, you know. Family business."

"Yes, I certainly do!"

"It's the vet Cliff hired before he died. Dutton Harris, who's managing the practice. Bringing someone in from the outside isn't always easy."

"No, I bet it isn't. I probably do understand some.

You know what Alan went through last year working at Equine Pharmaceuticals."

"That's why I can discuss the situation with you more than anyone else."

"Good."

"By the way, I suspect that revolver could be pretty rare. It's close to a hundred years old, and it has an octagonal barrel. It also says, *Made for Smith & Wesson. By Rollin White, Arms Co. Lowell, Mass.* on the top flat. I don't know the true significance of that, but I bet there *is* some. It's got a brass frame too, which is unusual. And it's also a seven shot, not the usual six."

"Meg! How do you know about guns?"

"I don't know much about antique guns, but I've been shooting all my life. I was taught by my aunt, which is kind of an interesting story, and Michael and I now, when we can actually find time, we still shoot targets over by the river. I may be seventy-six, Jo, but I do still have interests." Meg laughed.

And Jo held up her hands. "I know, I know—"

"Lots of folks figure when you're in your seventies all you're fit to do is sit on a porch and snap beans. Perhaps being raised in the military makes shooting seem like an ordinary hobby. I don't know, but I do enjoy it. And it's good to do something that's fun for Michael that gets him away from work."

Meg MacInnes spent the rest of that day typing up letters of recommendation for Nancy Petrosky and calling up vets she knew to give her an introduction, trying to prepare them to appreciate her abilities and not be surprised by her appearance. She drove the letters over to Nancy's house just before dinner.

And the next day Meg called more friends—people who owned or managed barns all around Lexington, as well as folks she knew at Keeneland Racecourse, and two tack stores in town.

Saturday, she went to see Dutton Harris. She'd arranged to meet him at the clinic, and she told him as professionally as she could that though she had no intention of interfering after he'd made the decision about Nancy—that that would be an improper intrusion by ownership into management's affairs—she did very much disagree with the decision he'd made.

She told him Nancy had potential and a work ethic and deep dedication that would have made her more than willing to work hard to gain more knowledge and meet his standards of instruction. She said employees who'd worked with them as long and faithfully as Nancy deserved consideration, and she'd appreciate it if, in the future, he contemplated terminating any other of their oldest employees that he'd consult with her first and give her an opportunity to be involved in the final decision.

Dutton Harris listened. He nodded politely and seemed to agree.

But Meg left without any real conviction that she could count on him doing what she'd asked.

CHAPTER TWO

Monday, February 23rd, 1965

The reaction wasn't long in coming. Three days after
Glenn Cook had met with his lawyer, and taken the
photographs of the confession and the valuables to the
Woodford County sheriff, after he'd put all the artifacts
and the original confession in a safety deposit box in his
bank in Versailles, after he'd sent photographs of everything they'd found to the Freemantle family (Samuel,
Marcella, Ronnie and his mother), Glenn was unlock-
ing his new front door so he could see what the
carpenters had gotten done—when Samuel Freemantle
braked his car in a shower of new-laid gravel and
climbed out with outrage flaming across his face.

"Sam! How are you?" Glenn was swiveling toward
him on his front porch, telling himself to smile.

"You have the audacity to ask me how I am? When
you've confiscated my rightful possessions and sullied
the reputation of my family!" Sam Freemantle was red

faced and sweating, his indistinct eyebrows raised in irritation, his midsection, in a clinging golf shirt, hanging over his old worn belt in a soft wide roll of fat.

"Now wait a minute, Sam—"

"*You* wait a minute! How do I know you haven't kept other pieces of silver and jewelry hidden away for yourself?"

"How?" Glenn had worked for army intelligence in Berlin in the late fifties, and the look on his face made Sam reconsider before he said another word. Glenn waited and watched and eventually spoke slowly in a deep steady voice that seemed to hold more menace than if he'd chosen to shout. "First of all, I've told you that's all I found. Secondly, Jo Munro and Meg MacInnes were here when we uncovered the artifacts and can corroborate what I've said."

Samuel Freemantle shoved his hands in his pockets and let out a shallow breath. "Alright. Maybe so. I still want to see the wall."

"It's down. If you want to come in and look at where it was, I'm willing to let you."

"That's the least you can do!"

"Is it?" Glenn looked at him with iron in his eyes and considered saying what he thought of him in general, as well as at that moment in particular—but he knew it wouldn't do either one of them any good. So he just led Sam through the hall and the dining room into what had been the sitting room and was about to become his bedroom.

They both stood in silence for a moment—Sam turn-

ing to take in the whole room, unpainted still and empty
—before he forced a gruff laugh, contemptuous sounding
and skeptical too, as he walked back to the hall. "You
think you're something, don't you?"

"I beg your pardon?"

"You had no right to send copies to the rest of the
family, *or* hold on to the original materials—that all
should've come to me as soon as you found it! I was the
former owner of the house and the direct descendent of
the Isaiah Freemantle who owned it in the 1800s."

"I expect you *are* the person it will go to when the
sheriff and the lawyers get through it all. My lawyer told
me to do what I did, and I stand by that decision. Putting
the valuables in a safety deposit box while the legal issues
are settled is my responsibility as the present owner of this
property and the person who found the cache. And if I
were a member of your family, I'd want copies too, so I'd
know I was being kept informed. The sheriff agreed with
the steps I was proposing, and I'm not about to apologize, or make any changes now."

"Aren't you? And after I let you have this house for
hardly more than a song!" Sam was breathing fast,
shuffling toward the porch.

Glenn let that go without a word. He just limped
behind him toward the front door. "I'm sorry you find
this as upsetting as you do. I was trying to act responsibly
in a very unexpected situation."

"I can see you've never met Marcella. What you've
done has created a state of unprecedented animosity, and

led to an outpouring of public humiliation that's become nearly unbearable!"

Sam was down the steps then, slamming his car door, as Glenn stood just inside the hall shaking his head as he watched.

Excerpt from Jo Grant Munro's Journal
Friday, March 19th, 1965

It's taken a month to see how it would all end up, but Meg was absolutely right about how Samuel and Marcella would react to what we found in the wall. Marcella's gotten herself interviewed by the Lexington <u>and</u> the Woodford County papers, and she's been trying to get herself on local TV. Ronnie donated copies of everything to the historical society that's just getting started, so that was good. But unfortunately, for the state of their souls, Samuel and Marcella have been seen scratching and spitting inside the Biscuit & Bacon, which gave the general populous a long looked for diversion.

Samuel, who must've been destined from the cradle to be the accountant he's become, is trying to sell whatever artifacts will make a buck, since it's all come to him as you'd expect. The Blanchard silver is worth more than any of us imagined, but Samuel still seems to be spending an inordinate amount of time complaining that Glenn gave photos of the confessions and the artifacts to others besides himself.

Human nature. Endlessly entertaining. Rich with cautionary tales.

"Mike!" Dutton Harris had slammed the door of his Ford pickup, and was walking toward the side door of MacInnes Equine Veterinary Services, just as Michael MacInnes headed toward his own truck with his arms full of supplies. "Could I talk to you for a second?" Dutton had turned back toward Michael, his rubber boots splattered with mud, his khaki pants and tweed jacket still clean and crisp.

Michael said, "Sure. I'm on my way to the Ingersol farm to float teeth and give a few shots, but I've got time," as he set two buckets on the gravel drive.

"I've had an estimate on repairing the clinic roof from Red Barn Roofing that I thought was reasonable, and they're planning to start week after next. Would you mind telling your mother? It's not something we need to discuss in person, but I want to keep her informed. Meg does still own the business, as we all know." Dutton chuckled and adjusted his tie, then started toward the employee door.

"Didn't you two talk about replacing the whole roof?"

"It was mentioned once a few weeks ago, but that would cost many times more, and it makes much better sense to put that off as long as we can."

Michael nodded at one of the assistants, who was rolling a wheelbarrow load of hay toward the recovery barn, while he told Dutton he'd tell his mom. "One thing I wanted to mention too, the last shipment of bandages from the new supplier aren't holding up. We're

having to throw a lot of them out, and I thought maybe
—"

"They're a fraction of the cost of the old ones, and
even if we have to discard some, we still come out ahead."

"Except that they shred. They get lint in the wounds.
Even when—"

"I'm in a rush right now, Mike. Could we talk about
it tomorrow perhaps?"

"Sure. Whenever you have a minute." Michael
watched Dutton disappear through the clinic's side door,
then pulled up the lid he'd had made by a welder to
cover the bed of his pickup. He'd had a carpenter build a
series of drawers and cabinets in the truck bed to hold the
equipment he had to take on farm visits, and he set his
stainless-steel buckets in their compartment, and stowed
two equine dental rasps in a drawer beside it. He arranged
syringes and drugs in their own drawers, and refastened
the lid.

Then he shook his head at a bony-looking broodmare, who was hanging hers in the back paddock, and
climbed behind the wheel.

Six hours later, Michael drove up the long drive from
McCowan's Ferry Road and took the left-hand branch
where it split at the bottom of the north-south hill on Jo
and Alan's farm. He turned left at the top, running
straight along the wide ridge, past paddocks and barns on
both sides, till the ridge met the ravine at the south end
of the property, and the drive curved to the right.

He drove toward the long side of Jo's rental cabin, where the original one-room pioneer house, with a low-ceilinged loft above, had become the south end of a much-enlarged cottage when Jo grafted another cabin onto the north end. The main entrance was now in the middle of the long east hall, under a cedar-shake shed roof, that connected the original house to a big new kitchen and living space in back.

Michael parked in the gravel east of the side door, but as he walked toward Meg, who'd opened the door and was grinning at him, he told himself one last time that he had to tell her, and now was the time, even if it made her worry.

They walked through the kitchen that opened out to the sitting room in back, with Meg's long-haired corgi, Jessie, trotting close to Michael, Meg moving like something hurt, even though she was trying hard to make herself ignore it.

March had started off cool in Kentucky, and Meg had lit a fire, and they sat on either side of the big stone fireplace, while logs collapsed and smoldered, and flames and sparks shot skyward, in a quiet, darkening night, the fragrance of wood smoke taking them both back to childhood, soothing their brains and their bones.

Meg had brought coffee and oatcakes she'd baked that afternoon, and she was watching Michael the way she had since he'd been born, knowing somewhere underneath her ribcage that something was coming that wasn't good news, while he talked about his dog, Wolf, and the gelding he was training.

She set her mug down on the side table by her straight-backed chair when he picked up another oatcake, and folded her hands in her lap. "Something's wrong at the clinic. I know you, Michael. You came with something to say."

Michael pinned his dark curly hair on top of his head with his hands for half a second, then leaned back and stretched his legs straight out beside the fire. "It's tricky. You need to know what Ronnie and I know, but if you say something to Dutton it puts both of us in an awkward position. If he sees us as spies, he might start covering up the changes he's making, and you need to know what he's doing. You know how Dad did things."

"I do."

"He bought the highest quality drugs and supplies, because patient care came before anything else. Everything except honesty. In a Thoroughbred culture that doesn't always care what corners get cut."

"How bad is it?"

"He says he's decided to repair the roof instead of replacing it."

"I told him two weeks ago I wanted it replaced."

"He got a repair quote, and says he's going ahead. He told me to tell you, so in that, at least, you can talk to him directly."

"What else?" She fingered one of her round gold earrings (the ones she wore every day of her life) without looking as though she'd noticed, while she stared at

Michael's broad-boned face, tight looking now and worried.

"He's buying bandages that fall apart a sizeable percentage of the time. He's buying out-of-date human drugs that are used for equines, yes, and with some drugs the standards are acceptable, and that's perfectly okay. In other cases it isn't. Ronnie organizes the inventory, and he can see how the standards are slipping."

"We can't let that go on."

"No. Ronnie still does the maintenance on our equipment too—the heating and cooling and that sort of thing—but also the X-ray and surgical equipment, the same way he did for Dad, and Dutton's postponing the routine servicing that needs to be done. He says the manufacturers schedule it way too soon to help their bottom line and he won't let them get away with it."

"That's preventative maintenance!"

"I agree."

Meg sat, gazing at the fire, holding her mug of coffee in her lap. "Is it all penny-wise-and-pound-foolish sorts of things? Or is there something more?"

"I don't know. As far as I know for sure, it's those kinds of cheapskate, short-sighted mistakes, but there're a couple of other areas I'm concerned about, even though I don't know enough to say."

"And?"

"He let Rachel go this week. The last vet assistant Dad trained. And brought in someone he'd worked with in the practice he worked for in Louisville."

"What reason did he give?"

"He said this Webber guy has years more experience in Thoroughbred breeding, and he wants an assistant when he goes out on the farms who's really seasoned. Somebody big and beefy to help handle the stallions. Yet *I* think we're understaffed, and Rachel could've stayed—especially since he let Nancy go. Folks are having to work too many hours when we've got ER patients coming into the clinic."

Meg nodded and sipped her coffee, then sighed and shook her head. "I've tried not to be the kind of owner who can't let go. You know, the ones who interfere, and hang on way too long. I trained Sara to manage the office, and I left as soon as I could after Cliff died. Dutton was trying to get his feet under him as the managing vet, and I thought it was the right thing to do."

"It was. You did it exactly right."

"I go into the office to examine the previous month's books by the tenth of every month, and I try to communicate with Dutton in a frank, polite, professional manner. But I will not let the clinic's quality of care suffer. Especially when Dutton's contract gives him the right to start buying a minority percentage of our shares come this September. No, he's been here almost eighteen months. This needs to get sorted out, one way or the other."

"It does. Absolutely."

"The roof's straightforward. The quality issues, without mentioning what I've heard from you, are a good deal more difficult. You know he'll assume that you've talked to me with any issue I raise."

"And then he could cut me off more than he does now." Michael's dark-blue eyes glanced at Meg's, and away again, but she saw the frustration and the anger.

"How is he cutting you off?"

"He limits me to routine work, except maybe a colic he thinks won't turn out well. Floating teeth. Giving inoculations. Everyday deworming. It makes sense, to a large degree. I'm newly qualified. I don't have the experience to run the practice, and I have no desire to, with what I know now. But right in his hiring agreement it says Dutton will include me in decision-making discussions, and mentor me as the future owner. I did more than a year of postgraduate pathology with Elvis Doll at UK, and Dutton won't even tell me about his cases. And the fertility work that was Dad's specialty, that Dad was training me to take over, Dutton's taking all that as well. He uses Jerry as his backup vet much more than me, and just sends me out on what's routine, or maybe doomed to failure."

They looked at each other in silence for a minute, before Meg said, "If Jerry had the kind of personality that welcomes responsibility rather than avoids it, Cliff might not have had to bring Dutton in as the managing vet."

"And yet, Dutton's references were good, and he interviewed really well. Dad had no reason to think it was a mistake. Or that he'd die himself six months later."

"I think we did the best we could, with what we knew at the time."

"I think you did too. If Rory and his wife hadn't gone back to Ireland everything would've been fine. I know! Her parents weren't well. And if wishes were horses—"

"Beggars would ride. I'll have to do something, Michael. Though what I don't know. I shall pray for insight, and hope I get some."

"By the way, do you know where Dad's handwritten notes are on all his fertility work? He kept notes on every case, and kept them at home, after they'd been typed and filed in each patient's file at the clinic. Copies went in his big fertility research file, and I can't find it at the office. I'm beginning to wonder if Dutton took it out of circulation."

"Why would Dutton do that?"

"I don't know. But I'm giving it some thought."

"Cliff's notes must be here somewhere. They were definitely at home when he died. The handwritten ones, and a set of the typed ones, if I remember correctly. I haven't gone through his papers yet. I packed everything up when I moved here, and haven't looked through the boxes. It's kind of peculiar, what I've sorted through, and what I still haven't."

"You went through his clothes right away."

"And his tack, when I gave you Carrick, and his carpentry tools too, most of which I gave to you. How's Carrick doing? I ought to go see him and take him some carrots."

"He's fine. He likes not having to work."

"I haven't wanted to go through Cliff's papers. Or his lap desk either one."

"You think the fact that the desk was with him in his truck when he died has something to do with it?"

"I s'ppose it could. I don't really understand why I've reacted the way I have."

"No?"

"No. That's not altogether true." A small soft smile came and went, before she spoke again. "I gave him that lap desk when he and I became engaged. I thought it was beautiful. It was early nineteenth century English. Walnut veneer and finely inlaid brass. And yet I knew very well I couldn't afford it. I was working as a secretary in a department store in Atlanta, and I had to scrimp on streetcar money, and do without lunch a good bit too, but I thought it would be so helpful to him when he went on his farm visits. He could write up his notes in his truck, and keep his invoices organized, and he used it as though it worked well for him the whole time we were married."

Meg smiled again, broader this time, more like her normal grin. And then she smoothed her dark-blue skirt and drank the last of her coffee. "All those years, he kept the letters I wrote him while we were engaged in an inside compartment underneath the writing surface— mine, along with two others from his oldest friend. Gordon was killed in World War I, and all Cliff had to remember him by were his last letters."

"I never heard a word about the letters."

"No, I don't s'ppose you did. I know I need to look through the lap desk. But I can't hardly bring myself to do it. It's as though it'd be the final severance. I know that's nothing remotely logical. But the time hasn't come."

"Then I say you shouldn't worry about it."

"I will look for the fertility files though. And I'll try very hard to talk to Dutton in whatever way I can that will leave you uninvolved."

Michael said, "What do you know about Nancy? Last I heard she was interviewing for a job at a dog kennel."

"She's working there three days a week, helping with the dogs and doing some cleaning, and two days a week at a nursing home, cleaning there too. Neither one of them are what she wants, so she's still applying other places, and I'm trying to help as well."

"I've been asking around at the barns I visit, but so far nothing's turned up."

Saturday, March 20th, 1965

"Thank you for coming on such short notice." Meg MacInnes led Dutton Harris through the entry hall, on through the kitchen, to the oval mahogany table beside the wide window in the east-facing dining area of the large white sitting room.

The table was set with sterling silver and blue-and-white china, and she poured freshly squeezed orange juice into crystal glasses, with water and coffee waiting in pitchers on the table. Then she brought in creamed curried chicken in homemade pastry shells, with bowls of freshly sliced pineapple.

"You didn't have to go to all this trouble, Margaret." Dutton smoothed his napkin in his lap and smiled across at Meg, his good-looking face unreadable as usual, while the brown eyes under smooth blond hair seemed to be studying Meg's.

"I enjoy cooking for someone besides myself, and I thought it might be fun to have brunch together while we discuss a couple of ideas I've had about the clinic."

"It *will* be fun. Thank you. I don't often get a home-cooked meal." Dutton ate a forkful of chicken and vegetables, and then poured coffee for Meg.

Meg asked about the most interesting cases, the kinds of surgeries he'd been able to do, and how particular horses were doing from farms where she knew the owners. She asked about research at Pennsylvania University's equine center, and what new antibiotics were coming out—before she got to what she had to say.

"It was very important to Clifford to maintain the facilities at a very high level—the building, the pastures, the equipment, both the physical plant and the medical equipment. It was equally important to him to use medical supplies of the highest possible quality, and just before he died he was talking about assigning a team of folks to monitor and oversee those areas at the clinic.

"He'd mentioned giving Ronnie Holmes oversight of the equipment and facilities, and asking Jerry and one of the assistants to oversee the quality control of the drugs and everyday supplies. Jerry, as a vet, the medications and surgical supplies. The tech, the general office supplies, and perhaps gloves and syringes and that sort of thing. It would keep Cliff from having to spend his own time involved in those areas, and would give the ones involved a team to work with to evaluate how they were performing. A sort of quality control group to help and challenge each other. He saw it as a way to develop our folks, and perform useful functions for the clinic. And it occurred to me last week, when I was looking over the books, that this might be a really good time to implement his approach."

"Purchasing is responsible for a very large percentage of our practice expenditure, and doing that practically—being able to negotiate good pricing, buying based on magnitude of scale—all of that takes training and experience. We're not a large practice. We're competing against practices like Hagyard here, and Harthill in Louisville. We can't afford to purchase solely on quality. There are grades of acceptable materials that we can use very appropriately, and keep our overhead as low as is practical."

"I realize that. I'm not suggesting we always buy the very most expensive materials, but quality has to come first. It makes economic sense too in the long run. Our clients pay for what we supply them, and if what we supply gives them value for their money, it works out for all of us."

"I think it's a more complicated situation than you may realize."

"Michael did tell me, by the way, as you asked him to, that you're hoping to patch the roof instead of replace it. You and I did agree to replace it, and I have to say I think it's important that we do. I know Cliff would have done that, and I think the Worthington Roofing quote was reasonable. We don't have to do the prep barn, or the recovery barn, only the labs and offices, and the OR, of course, and I—"

"That will adversely affect our operating income. I don't know if you realize—"

"I've examined the books every month, Dutton, and I think it's a justified expenditure. We're sitting on enough cash to warrant that kind of expense, and roofs are notorious. Repairing leads to more and more leaks and troubles down the road."

They were both quiet for a minute, eating chicken and pastry, drinking orange juice and coffee—while avoiding each other's eyes.

"You own the business, Margaret. If you're determined to replace the roof, we'll certainly replace it. I haven't signed the repair contract, so there's no insurmountable problem."

"Good. And what do you think about the quality team? Letting Ronnie take responsibility for mechanical repairs and updates. And Jerry take on medications, and maybe Sara or Irene oversee our supplies?"

"If you're bound and determined to insist on that approach, we'll adopt it. But I don't think it's wise. None of them is trained in purchasing, and they won't make wise decisions."

"I'm inclined to pursue it in some way. Why don't you think about it too, and let's discuss how we could approach it, perhaps sometime next week?"

"We can do that. I'll be gone Thursday, returning late on Friday, so Jerry and Michael will be working extra hours. Golden Window Farm is flying one of their best breeding stallions down to Florida to breed there and they've hired me to accompany him to make sure nothing goes wrong on the flight. It's Night Captain. He's a bit of a rogue, and he has a long history of being nervous in the air."

"Then let's hope it goes well."

"Yes. I'm sorry to rush off, but I need to go, Meg. I've got a social engagement in Louisville this evening, and paperwork to finish first. Thank you for lunch. I appreciate it."

"You're welcome. Let's talk again next week."

Meg watched Dutton, from the east door, as he climbed into his Jaguar XKE, low to the ground and indisputably gorgeous, with the top folded down. Jessie watched with her—the highly intelligent, opinionated corgi Meg had rescued after a good friend who'd raised Jessie had died six months before.

She was generally very friendly, but she had her aversions, and Dutton Harris appeared to be one of them. For Jessie sat, like a gold-and-white bottle brush, huge ears pointed straight up, and growled quietly deep in her throat, even after Meg closed the wide glass door.

CHAPTER THREE

Tuesday, April 13th, 1965

It was a small farm, thirty miles south of Lexington, owned by a several-generation farm family that couldn't make a living off the land anymore. The husband worked in a factory in Lexington. The wife worked as a cook in the cafeteria at a local elementary school. Their only daughter had one horse that meant more to her than most people, even in the horse world, get to experience firsthand.

They could rarely pay their vet bills in one lump sum, so Cliff and Margaret had let them (and a good many others) pay a little at a time. And when Susie's gelding, Whiskers, had come up lame, Carl Miller called MacInnes Equine and asked them to send Michael MacInnes to come take a look.

Which meant Michael had to pack up the portable X-ray. It weighed eighty-five pounds, and the plates were large, heavy and cumbersome, but having a portable X-ray of any kind had transformed equine care, and it got used in the clinic, and out on the farms, several times a day.

When Michael was loading his truck, Ronnie Holmes came out the side door and asked if he could go with him. Calibrating the X-ray machine after its last repair wasn't as straightforward as it'd been, and he'd like to be part of the set-up and observe for himself how it performed in the field.

"Sure. I'll get the plates. You grab the machine."

They both laughed, before Ronnie said, "Nice try," and picked up the plates himself. "You've been pullin' that since you were six!"

Whiskers was an Appendix Quarter Horse (half-Thoroughbred, half-Quarter Horse), who was fine-boned for having Quarter Horse blood, and not more than fifteen hands, a chestnut with a white blaze and a white hind foot.

He was quiet and well behaved, and his eleven-year-old owner held his lead rope as though she knew he barely needed one as Michael palpated his front left leg. There was swelling and tenderness along the inside of the cannon bone between the fetlock and the knee, in the lower third, primarily, closer to the fetlock. There was no visible external wound, and Michael was reasonably sure it was an injury to the small inside splint bone that lay along the big cannon bone, usually caused by an over-extended fetlock when that leg is bearing weight. Which would mean it was nothing, if all went well, that would make Whiskers permanently lame.

Only an X-ray could confirm that, and Michael and Ronnie took six from all sides of the foreleg. It was time-consuming, and Whiskers had to hold still for much longer than he would've had to only a few years later—but he did hold still, because he'd been trained, and clearly trusted Susie.

While Michael pulled the X-ray away and began to wrap up the cord, Susie slid her hand down Whiskers's neck and started to play with his mane. "Whiskers didn't seem lame when I saw him trot in the paddock day before yesterday, but he looked off at the canter. And when I rode him later he didn't feel real normal even at the trot. It was yesterday morning I saw some swelling on the inside up above his fetlock, so I put ice on him a couple of times, and kept him in his stall."

Michael said, "That's exactly what you should've done. There's no open wound, so we don't have to worry about infection, and the splint bone doesn't feel like it's moved much out of place. But the X-ray'll tell us for sure. Sometimes the outside splint can be traumatized too even if it doesn't swell. But I'll put a pressure bandage on him, and you just keep him on stall rest, and I'll let you know as soon as Ronnie here gets the plates developed."

"Unless there's some kind of emergency at the clinic, I'll get it done by tomorrow."

"Thank you." Susie rubbed Whiskers's chin, and he closed his eyes and sighed. "Mom and Dad couldn't get here to talk to you from work, but you know how we used to pay a little at a time?" She blushed first, and then looked right at Michael. "The last time, when Whiskers had hives and we had to have Dr. Harris, he said we'd have to pay everything from then on all at once, and Dad's been thinkin' that—"

"No, you don't. I'll talk to Dr. Harris. Don't you worry about it. Your folks and I'll decide how much you pay every month. You take really good care of Whiskers. Lots of folks, with a lot more money, can't be bothered. You've always paid right on time, and there's no reason that should change."

"Thank you. We was pretty worried." She looked as though she was hoping she wouldn't blush again as she led Whiskers into his stall and pulled off his halter and lead rope.

Ronnie Holmes was looking out the passenger window on the drive back to the clinic, while he wiped barn dust off his black-framed glasses with the front of his blue cotton shirt. He wasn't good looking. Not like Michael —or even Dutton, with his slick Ivy League cuff links and his perfectly manicured hair. Ronnie was a farm kid who'd served in Korea, and come back with shrapnel on one side of his forehead. Ronnie's face was thin and kind of lopsided, his nose long and bony, his eyes small and gray and close together and deep set under irregular brown eyebrows. It was a serious face, especially now, when he was trying to explain to Michael how work was making him worry.

"I'm still doing the inventories, though how long Dutton'll let me I don't know. And you know, with the nonprescription meds it can be hard to be precise. The skin treatments. The alcohol rubs. The vitamins and the supplements. But there're too many times when he says he's treated a horse with something, that the inventories don't match.

"I'm trying to keep my own separate records to compare over time, but I'm beginning to think he'll write a treatment on a client's bill that he didn't actually do. Not when he's meeting face-to-face with a client, but out at the small private barns, where the owners are at work, and there's nobody there to meet him, and he goes in and treats the horse completely on his own."

"That's disgusting." Michael glanced at Ronnie, with a cold hard lump in his chest.

"Yep. And there's somethin' else that seems kinda fishy. You ever heard of furosemide?"

"Just recently. For the first time. You know, I try to read human medical journals to see what's coming down the pike, because some orthopedic techniques can be translated to equines, and some human drugs can be used on horses as well. Anyway, I read a translation of a German journal article that talked about furosemide having been synthesized a couple of years ago—1962, if I remember right. It's a diuretic. It reduces fluid retention in the body. They're thinking of using it for heart patients like you'd expect."

"Well, just before the races at Keeneland, this package came in from Germany for Harris. I put it in supply, like I always do, and told him it was there. It didn't look like a normal commercial kinda product. It was like somebody'd taken a liquid from another bottle and poured it into this one, and sealed it up by hand, and stuck on a handwritten label."

"That's interesting."

"Yeah. Well, it sat there on the shelf, and then when Dutton went to the races at Keeneland to care for that horse from Louisville that was runnin', he took the bottle with him. I don't know nothin' about what you could use it for, but the bottle never came back. And I wondered if he dosed that horse at the track."

"I don't know what you could do with it that would help a racehorse run faster. Not right off the top of my head. But I can sure do some more research. It'd make a horse lose some water weight. But you'd think it could cause some dehydration too, and that wouldn't be good."

"Just thought you oughtta know."

"I'm really glad you told me. I've run into strange things too. You know how you have to declare that a horse has been pin fired for a bowed tendon before you race, so the bettors can take that into account? Dutton filed a report at Churchill Downs on a three-year-old mare in Louisville last week saying he'd fired her last August. When I looked at her actual file, there's no record that he fired her. And no record that she was injured, or that he ordered stall rest, and then hand walking the way you would. Heck, I gave her her shots in

November and there was no sign of firing then. But the owner's a guy he's known for a long time. Someone I've seen him out to dinner with. And it's making me plenty nervous. Is Dutton a lousy record keeper? Or is he helping out his friend? The mare could potentially perform better than expected with that on her record, running at lower odds, than she might otherwise, and the owner could benefit, and any other bettor as well."

"Can you imagine what your dad would say!"

"Yeah. And what do I do about it? We need an experienced older vet running this practice. The two big practices we're competing against, their senior partners are really well known, and with Dad gone it's a whole lot harder than it was to hold our own. But if we get real evidence of wrong doing, Mom'll let him go, I know that, but it'll still be a blow. Especially with the big barns, and when they're racing at Keeneland and Churchill Downs, and during the sales too."

"So whatta we do?"

"Pay attention to anything that seems odd and start taking notes. Mom found Dad's fertility case studies and I'm going over those, and even though it's really early days, there're some very interesting indications there."

"That's not all that's going on in my life either. Not at the clinic, but—"

"What d'you mean?"

"'Member cousin Sam, and the stuff Glenn found in the wall?"

"Yeah."

"Well, Sam's sold the gun to some collector for alotta

money, and he's selling the cups and the rest of the silver to all kinds of folks, and he's blabbing about how much he's getting to everybody in the family, and prob'ly a large part of central Kentucky, and my Aunt Marcella, she's furious and phoning Mom in the middle of the night, and me too when Mom doesn't answer at her house, and it's making Mom crazy. What's wrong with people? Life's too short."

"Yeah, well, that's a very good question."

Ronnie could see the car in his driveway halfway down the block. He knew whose it was too, and he groaned before he swore—Marcella, in her bright red Ford, crouching behind the wheel.

He decided not to pull in behind her because the last thing he wanted to do was delay her departure, so he parked in the street in front of his small clapboard ranch and told himself to remain calm no matter what she did.

She was standing by the driver's door by the time he'd gotten out of his truck and said, "Hey. What are you doin' out here? How come you didn't go in?"

"I got nothin' whatever to say to your wife! You oughtta know that by now." Her hair was dyed a new shade of red, and her eyebrows were penciled-in in high red arcs. Her wrinkled skin looked clogged with makeup and her lipstick, in an alarming shade of orange, had seeped into the cracks around the tight line of her lips. She was wearing a red plaid skirt and a flowered vest over a pale blue blouse, and her shoes were worn and very high heeled and her feet looked swollen and sore. "Get in the car so we can talk."

"Why don't we stand here so—"

"I don't want the world listenin'."

Ronnie looked at her for a half a second, seeing the fevered, frantic, agitation flowing through her whole body, and decided it made the most sense to accommodate whatever he could of the many demands that were coming. "Fine. I'll get in the car, but I'm rollin' down the window. I been hot all day."

She was almost screaming by the time she'd closed the door, her face splotchy, her eyes red-rimmed, her forehead clenched tight. "Sam's got every single piece of silver and jewelry, and you won't lift a finger! You and your mother, who's avoided takin' a stand as long as I can remember. *His* ancestor committed the murder! He shouldn't be the one to benefit from the crime!"

"The valuables belonged to his ancestors who *didn't* commit the crime. It was the—"

"You know how much that silver's worth? It should-da come to us! And you don't even give a damn that *our* ancestor was wrongly accused, and slandered across Kentucky, and dragged all the way to court when he was the one who was innocent!"

"Marcella, it was close to a hundred years ago, and I don't see the—"

"*Now* we've got a chance to publicly right that wrong, and you won't talk to the press, or do the first little thing that would—"

"I've given the Woodford County Historical Society

a copy of the confession, and pictures of everything that was found in the wall. I've told them they can do a display when they open their doors next fall, and that's enough for me."

"Well, it's not enough for me, I can tell ya that right now. You know how much a lawyer'll cost to go after Sam and get back what belongs to us? And you won't contribute a penny to put this wrong right!"

"And I bet that's what bothers you most."

"Don't you get smart with me! I always knew you were weak kneed, but I didn't know you were in Sam's pocket!" She was shaking, clutching the steering wheel, her skirt skooched up exposing part of one leg of her dingy-looking panty girdle, her big red earrings quivering underneath her earlobes.

"I'm sorry it bothers you as much as it does, but I got nothin' else to say." Ronnie opened the door, and had just climbed out and turned around to close it, when she threw an empty paper cup out the door behind him.

Wednesday, April 14th, 1965

"Michael." Dutton called to him from his dad's old office as Michael walked into the small one next door that he shared with Jerry Rineholt. "Could you come in here, please?"

"Sure."

"I assume your mother spoke to you about her idea

for a team that would oversee the quality of our supplies."

"Briefly. After she mentioned it to you, I think."

"Really." Dutton was twirling a pencil in a circle on
his desk, while contemplating Michael with a cool
appraising eye. "I don't agree with her approach. I have,
however, investigated the bandages and dressings you
found unsatisfactory, and I've found another supplier who
seems to offer higher quality at a moderately higher price.
I'd like you to tell Ronnie to ship the last shipment back,
once the new stock arrives."

"Sure."

"It would be more professional if you spoke to me
rather than your mother whenever you have concerns."

"I did speak to you."

"And not your mother?" Dutton was smiling con-
descendingly, leaning back in his chair, locking his fingers
together on the top of his head. "There's a colic case at
Applewood Farm you need to take care of. It doesn't
sound good."

Michael nodded and stepped into the long hall that
ran along the operating room, out to the side door, thinking, *Why am I not surprised? A colic case that stands a good
chance of having to be put down.*

Dutton picked up his phone and dialed Meg MacInnes as
soon as Michael was out of earshot, tapping the eraser of
his pencil on his desk, while he waited for her to answer.

"Meg?… It's Dutton. I wanted you to know that I've

looked into Michael's concerns over the new supplier of bandages, and I think he makes a good point. They don't come up to the highest standards, though I wouldn't have expected that based on the catalogue and the salesman who called... Right. Yes. So I've found another supplier that's slightly more expensive but appears to offer a higher quality product, and I've ordered a first shipment from them. We'll send back the inferior materials as soon as the new ones arrive... Yes. Yes, that's exactly right... The quality team? No. I still don't think that's the right approach. It'd be opening a can of worms. But let's both think about it some more and talk another time... Yes. You too. Maybe next week."

Sara Fletcher, the office manager Meg had trained to take over her position, stuck her head in the door and told Dutton his mother was on the phone, and it was the third time she'd called that day.

"Tell her I'm busy, and she should try me at the weekend, and then only at home." He dropped the pencil in his center drawer and shoved his chair back from the desk. "I've got a breeding to do at Edgeware Farm and I'll be gone the rest of the day."

Michael MacInnes drove into his driveway a little before nine that night. It was just about dark, though the moon was splashing silver in patches across the paddocks, and the wind was blowing strips of cloud high and quick across a teal-gray sky.

Michael opened the gate by the road, locked it be-

hind him, parked in the garage attached to the breezeway, and went right over to Wolf, his big shepherd-
huskie mix, letting him out of his fifteen-by-fifteen
fenced-in pen with his two-room handmade house.

Wolf leapt and jumped and nuzzled his hands, and
Michael talked to him all the way to the paddock where
he went to get Drummond, his big bay gelding, while his
dad's old horse, Carrick, ran the fence-line, trumpeting
and leaping and jumping, telling Michael he'd wanted to
go in for quite some time already.

Once Drum was on his way to the barn, Wolf ran
into his paddock, and jumped two horse jumps for his
own amusement, then raced back to catch up with
Michael when he came back to lead Carrick into his stall
in the barn.

A high-school kid who lived down the road had fed
them grain around six, and all Michael had to do was put
them in their stalls, refill their water buckets, and throw
them two flakes of hay.

He chased Wolf around for a few minutes, and then
told him he was hungry and needed to make his dinner.
"You wantta come in, or stay out for a while? It's up to
you. In or out. Just make up your mind now."

Wolf considered the open door from the breezeway
to the kitchen, his blue huskie eyes telling Michael his
decision, even before he went on through and parked
himself on his bed by the breakfast table in the small bay
window—where he watched Michael drop his briefcase
by the table, and go about making a sandwich.

There was dry food in Wolf's bowl, but he clearly

wasn't interested. He was thinking about licking the mixing bowl once Michael dished up his tuna.

He sat and stayed, once the bowl was put in front of him, till Michael said, "Okay," then he calmly polished the pottery with meticulous attention to detail.

Michael sat with his sandwich, and the rest of the can of tuna he'd mixed with mayonnaise and celery, with two glasses of V8 too, and two large ruby red grapefruit.

He picked up the phone, though, before he took a bite, and placed a call to Midway.

"Hey, Laura… I know. I just got home. How was your day?" He listened then to a day in the life of a woman who worked for Keeneland Racecourse in that very different world of public relations, and laughed some, and commiserated too, between bites of tuna and toast.

When it was his turn, he told her about his last five hours trying to save a ten-year-old mare who'd gone into colic after getting home from a show. How it'd ended the way he'd feared it would right from the beginning— when he put her down in her paddock, where burying her with a backhoe would be easier than anywhere else on the farm.

"How do I stand it?… I don't know. It's part of the job you can't get away from. And sometimes it's worse than others. If you know the horse, and you like it, and the owners really care about it, that's the hardest. When it's folks who see it in terms of money, I can sympathize because it's got to be a business for a lot of people, but it won't hit me the same way. My job is to treat the horse if

I can, try to reduce the suffering, evaluate the symptoms properly, and know when to call a halt. But when it's mild, and it goes really well, you know why you became a vet. It's funny, when you think about it. The horse finally poops, and all of us watching applaud. But if I can't cope with the hard parts, I'd better get another job.

"Dutton?... Not good. I've got the notes now from Mom on Dad's years of fertility work, so that's going to be interesting... Primarily because it seems to me that a couple of stallions I remember Dad telling me were permanently infertile, because of an injury or an early disease, Dutton is now claiming have gotten mares in foal under his brilliant breeding. I can't say that for sure yet, but I want to read through the notes at the very least...

"You think there's something else? You think you know me that well do you, to know when things are bothering me?" Michael laughed and finished his V8, then listened with a look on his face that would've reminded Meg of Michael when he was a little boy and his dad had hugged him, and picked him up, and told him he'd done something really well.

"Thanks. Yeah. But no, you're right. It's that I can't understand why Dutton put Night Captain down on that flight to Florida. I've worked with Captain in a couple of situations, and he seemed like a commonsensical guy. You know how some horses are just silly. They'll terrify themselves over nothing. And if they can find a way to hurt themselves, they will. And how others just seem to make good decisions. They don't tend to panic. They don't overreact to what's around them. He was like that.

I thought. And he'd been flown all over in his lifetime, racing and breeding both. And yet Dutton says he went berserk on the flight and he had to put him down... I don't know. Ten days or two weeks ago. But it's sticking in my craw...

"What would you think about Saturday? Supposedly I'm not on call... No, whatever you want... Sure. That sounds good. Go out, or stay in, it doesn't matter to me... So your mother wants us to pick the date, hunh. I can do that. Bearing in mind that weddings are women's work. Men need to shut their mouths and stay out of the way." He laughed again, and shoveled a section of grapefruit in his mouth with a serrated spoon.

"Yeah, I am tired. I'm going to get a shower and take Dad's notes to bed with me... You too. I love you, Laura. I'll talk to you tomorrow."

Wolf was watching every move Michael made, and when he put his plate down for Wolf to lick, it almost looked as though he smiled.

It was after eleven, and Michael had fallen asleep with the light on, and his dad's notes on his chest, but he woke himself up and rubbed his eyes, and started reading again.

It was half an hour later, when he sat up in bed, and used three words to describe Dutton Harris he'd hardly used since he'd gotten out of the army, in a voice that made Wolf sit up on his own bed and look Michael right in the eye.

CHAPTER FOUR

Excerpt from Jo Grant Munro's Journal
Sunday, April 18th, 1965

*Odd, really, what Buddy Jones ended up telling me when he
and his wife and the twins stopped over. They've just gotten
back from Aiken where he spent the winter working for Mack
Miller. Mack's definitely taken Buddy under his wing, and
he's traveling with Mack when he moves his owner's horses
south, and north, throughout the year, and it's been a real step
forward for Buddy.*

*Anyway, Ross and the twins had fun together, and then
while Becky was watching them, the way she used to do before
they moved, Buddy took me aside. He's got real respect for
Charlie Smalls, who's a stallion groom at Claiborne Buddy's
known for a good long while, and the last time he ran into
Charlie he told Buddy something about his cousin who works
for a barn up around Louisville. Seems like this cousin said*

something to him about hoping he'd never have to work with MacInnes Equine Vet Services again. Buddy knows Meg's renting our cabin, and he figured maybe she should know. At least that there's some kind of rumor floating around. That he'd want to know if he were her, and I would too.

I got the cousin's name, and I'll tell Meg about it, but it could be kind of hard to pursue. He's a Negro man who works for a small private barn, and he may be unwilling to talk for fear of losing his job. Gossiping in the horse business is a good way of committing suicide of one sort or another.

Monday, April 19th, 1965

Meg and Glenn Cook had waited till they thought he'd be home from work, then went to see the general manager of the big Irish stud farm that had bought her sixty-five acres. He lived in Meg's old house now, and when they talked to him on the front porch, he said it was fine with him for them to stay and take pictures, then offered them tea as well.

They declined. And he went in. And Glenn had been rambling all over ever since, a metal crutch clamped on his left arm to make him more stable on uneven ground, as he shot film in all directions.

Meg was watching him, when she wasn't gazing at the house she and Cliff had loved—the handmade brick and white trim, the dark-green shutters and double white doors under a peaked porch roof, the whole house looking like it'd grown out of the ground on the top of that hill—while she held the print in her hands.

She knew exactly what she wanted Glenn to paint. It was her favorite photograph of Cliff after they'd moved to Kentucky, taken years later when he was in his sixties, there on the lawn in front of the house, his right arm draped over Carrick's withers, Carrick cropping grass, his dark-bay coat shining in the sun and his lead rope loose on the ground, Cliff leaning against him, his right foot crossed across his left ankle, wearing old worn jeans and a pale-blue shirt, grinning at Meg who was taking the picture, teasing her about keeping her fingers off the camera lens.

Glenn had understood right away why she chose it for the painting. But he'd wanted to come and photograph the house, as well as the trees and boxwoods on the right, so he'd see how to use them to soften the edge of the frame.

He swiveled around and smiled at Meg, letting his camera hang from his neck, setting his aviator sunglasses on his nose, before he started swinging himself across the lawn toward her. "What would you think about a three-foot square? A horizontal rectangle would work well too. Maybe thirty inches high by thirty-six?"

"You're the only one who knows enough to make that decision." She was shading her eyes with her right hand, a high black belt cinching her blouse outside her long denim skirt, her smile wide and easy, making her look like Olivia de Havilland might in another twenty years.

They heard it first, a truck coming up the drive, stone dust billowing out behind it. It was Michael, pulling up behind her car in the circular drive, climbing out of the driver's door, slamming it hard behind him. "I was out on a farm call west of here and I figured I'd stop and say hello."

Meg said, "I'm glad you did. We could all go out to dinner, if you want to."

"I can't, Meg. But thanks." Glenn had put his camera in Meg's car, and was loosening the hinges on his knee brace, getting ready to climb in.

"I can't either. I've got to get back to the clinic. But I thought I might drop by later."

"Maybe we could take the dogs for a walk, if you stop and get Wolf on the way."

"I don't know if I'll have time. We'll see. Glad you're doing the painting, Glenn."

"Thanks. I am too."

Jenny, one of the assistants Cliff had trained, was on night duty that night. There was one surgical recovery, an ovariectomy that had gone well, and Jenny was watching TV in the bedroom they used for staff as well as owners of emergency cases, when Michael got to the clinic. She'd feed and water the long-term recovery patients in the back barn at ten, and check on everyone throughout the night, but she had free time in between, and she was watching a rerun of *Rawhide* and drinking a large Coke.

He chatted with her for a minute and said he probably wouldn't be long, that he had to get some cultures going, and do a couple of other things, and then he'd take off. Jerry was on call, and hopefully it'd be quiet.

He ran four cultures on the puncture wound he'd examined at the Wilson's barn, and arranged the petri dishes in the emptiest incubator.

Then he went into his office and typed up a one-page report. He put it into a new file, then took a list of dates out of his shirt pocket. He walked into the reception area next door to his office, and turned on a desk lamp rather than the overhead lights. He was trying to remember where the old appointment books were stored. He knew they kept them for five years, but in which cabinet or vertical file he wasn't at all sure. He opened cabinets, and pulled out drawers, trying to be quiet, trying to work quickly, and finally found them in the bottom drawer of the file by the back hall.

He took out the one from 1964, and picked up the current book from the desk, and carried them into his office.

He found what he was looking for in January through May of 1964—six visits by Dutton to Rain Tree Farm to breed the stallion Ebenezer for Walter Howser to six different mares, and two to another stallion at Rain Tree Farm, now deceased, called Vixer, during that spring. He looked at the rest of Dutton's schedule on those days. He took notes, and moved to the current appointment book, where he found more visits to Ebenezer. There were gaps in Dutton's schedule earlier during those days as well.

There were gaps in Dutton's schedule in the afternoon before he went to breed Francisco for Sam Acheson to two different mares on two different days in March, very late in the day, but there weren't the other coverings that same day that he'd thought he might find.

Michael put the books back in the reception area and picked up the file from his desk. He stood there for a minute, hearing himself breathe, thinking about contingencies that might make sense—*if* he had to come up with one.

He stepped into the back hall and opened the door into Dutton's office on the other side of his from reception. He turned on the desk lamp and looked for an appointment calendar, first in the stacks of files on the desk, then in the center drawer.

It was there—brown leather, deckle-edged, eight by ten, a week on every page.

He'd found the entries for March 1965, and had just seen the same blank spaces as the office book, when the overhead light flashed on.

"What are you doing in my desk!" Dutton was standing in the doorway to the back hall with white-hot fury on his face.

"I was looking to see if you have time to go out to the Wilson place late tomorrow, or early the day after, to see to Silver's shoulder wound, or whether I should put it in my schedule."

"That's not any of your—"

"I was called out there this afternoon, and my report's in this file. I wrote notes in the regular file too, and I took a sample from the wound and I've cultured it, and we should have some preliminary results late tomorrow. From what the owner said, it's done nothing but get worse, even with the injected antibiotic, the topical cream, and the pills. The infection's serious, and we've gotta change our approach."

Dutton stared at Michael without saying a word, and it looked to Michael as though he were tamping himself down, banking the fire inside, before letting himself speak. "Why didn't you consult the book in reception?"

"I did, but I was making sure you didn't have something else scheduled in your own book that hadn't been transferred to the main book, the way we all forget once in a while. It's a nasty wound, Dutton, deep in the muscle. It's still got to be left to drain. We can't suture it now. And if you have no objections, I'd actually like to take it on. But it's your call, and if you—"

"You may take the case if you wish. Of course, the treatment will end up costing more than the animal's worth."

"The owner bred him, and trained him, and rides him all the time, and he's worth a whole lot to her. Did you culture the wound before? I couldn't find it in the notes."

"I saw no reason in the early stages to go to that extreme. I take it you've finished in my office?"

"Yes. Yes. I apologize for looking at your appointment calendar, but—"

"I object to anyone going through my personal belongings, as I'm sure you can understand. I can also see that from your perspective your action may have been justified. Even so, I don't want there to be a repetition, for any reason whatsoever."

"No, I understand. I'll see you tomorrow." Michael moved his report on Silver's wound to the center of the desk and nodded to Dutton as he walked out into the hall.

Meg rotated her hips the way she always did before she took a walk, then stood on the top of the two shallow steps that led up to the original cabin—which Jo had made into a master bedroom with a small sitting room next door (where Meg had put her baby grand piano)—and let her heels hang down off the edge.

Her hips hurt from arthritis, from years of riding, and hiking all her life, from sitting too long at office work, from being thrown one last time by a friend's unreliable mare.

She was thinking about whether to take another aspirin, and what her friend Lily had gone through with her hips—when she rolled her eyes and said, "Stop!"

Everybody hurts at your age. You can walk a mile or two three days a week. You can swim. You can sit long enough to practice the piano, and play for the choir when they call you. Mama was dead by this time. And she'd lost three children, which I can't imagine, having lost only one.

Meg shook her head slowly, remembering her mother's and her daddy's last years, before she slung Jessie's leash over her shoulder, then opened the door and watched her rush into the night like a long-haired blond bolster. Jessie couldn't be trusted yet not to chase the mares and babies, and Meg always carried a leash in case she had to hold her back.

Meg was stiffer than sometimes, and she stretched again in her driveway, thinking about Glenn and what he had to put up with every day of his life. He'd been jumping a stone wall three years before, on land where he'd rented a house, when a deer shot out of the woods directly into their path panicking his gelding, who'd hit the wall and flipped over, just missing Glenn with his body, but hitting him hard with his head, where Glenn had landed on rocky ground.

Glenn had broken his left hip, and his pelvis, and his left leg in more than one place, but he'd recovered better than anyone expected, partly because his surgeon had invented several revolutionary techniques during World War II, including the metal brace he strapped on top of his clothes. It'd only been a year and a half since Glenn's last surgery, but he'd picked up his life and was getting along as well as anyone could. And he still went to visit his old horse a couple of times a month.

Meg saw then that Jessie was limping too, a little, from a thorn in a pad a couple of days earlier, as she started sneaking along a paddock fence as though she were thinking about ducking under. She came though, when she was called, and Meg told her how wonderful she was before she looked at the night.

It made her stop and inhale the scent of sundried grass and wild iris, and stare for half a minute too, gazing across that ridge, where the sun was a last low line of salmon stretched above the trees, and the wild purple redbuds were blooming the whole length of those western woods, where the dogwoods lit up scattered patches with a white that almost glowed.

Meg watched and hummed and listened to the yearlings blowing and snorting and wheeling on her right, till they'd almost gotten to Jo and Alan's house, where Meg saw Michael's truck coming up the long drive from the road down on her right. She snapped the leash on Jessie, and waited for Michael to stop, then she set Jessie on the bench seat and climbed in beside her, asking if he'd eaten.

"Not yet, no."

"I've got meatloaf left from dinner."

They didn't talk much while she made him a salad and heated up green beans with bacon, and a large slice of meatloaf. But when they'd sat down at the oval table by the east window in the big back room, Meg said, "What's going on, Michael? You were irritated about something when you stopped at the old house."

"Not you."

"No, I know. But something."

"I got called out to see a backyard horse, a nice old guy with no particular claim to fame, with a puncture wound in his shoulder that's now badly infected. Dutton's been treating him for over two weeks and it's gotten a whole lot worse. The owner's worried, and she asked for someone besides Dutton to come out. Dutton hasn't cultured the wound. He gave him antibiotics, but when he wasn't responding, he didn't culture. And he hasn't gone back the way he should've. Anyone can see that what he gave him isn't working, and I don't think he cares. And you can bet your bottom dollar that if this was an expensive Thoroughbred from one of the big farms, the treatment would've been better."

"What are we going to do, Michael? This is more than penny-wise-and-pound-foolish." Meg sat holding her glass of iced tea, staring at the worry on Michael's face.

"I know. And that's not all. I've waited till I've uncovered more to tell you, but Dad's notes on his infertility cases have led to some interesting findings. There're three stallions Dad said were sterile that Dutton claims have bred mares."

"There are certain conditions that can reverse themselves though, aren't there?"

"Sure. Too much Equipose. That's a preparation of testosterone they give when they're racing, thinking it'll make them run faster, that leads pretty often to infertility when they come off the track. That can reverse over time, even though it doesn't always."

"I remember your dad telling me some of them ended up doing just fine."

"But an occlusive benign tumor where it blocks the sperm from traveling both the sperm tracts, that doesn't reverse. And getting kicked, often when they're breeding a mare, that can do irreparable damage to the testicles."

"Getting caught on a fence? Or jumping a wall as well?"

"Yeah, that's exactly right." Michael finished his tea, then folded his arms across his middle. "Also a disease with long periods of high fever, one of the influenzas, or, in this case pneumonia, those are the conditions that compromised these horses and made them permanently infertile."

"And yet you're saying Dutton's claiming that he's successfully bred these stallions that your dad said are infertile?"

"Right. I've found the dates Dutton says he bred them last year, and this year as well. Nothing like a full breeding schedule, just individual breedings with the same mares, or the same owners. Owners he's known in all cases from when he was in Louisville. And I'm not buying it. Dad wasn't wrong about things like that."

"What would be the significance of that?"

"Good question. Two things occur to me. When he breeds these infertile stallions, the mares go to the stallion's barn, like you'd expect, but it's always late afternoon or early evening when he schedules these coverings. Maybe the stallion owner wants to be there. Or maybe there's another reason. But why are there always gaps in Dutton's schedule right before those coverings?"

"I have no idea."

"Let's say Dutton breeds another stallion on another farm, maybe even his own stallion, to another mare and collects the sperm. Maybe he does a whole collection with a condom. Or maybe he uses the sperm they collect at the end of the live cover on a stick-and-a-cup the way they do, and he takes it out to the infertile stallion's barn and uses it to artificially inseminate a mare so that it looks like the infertile stallion is actually throwing babies. It'd be easy for Dutton to use his stallion. Though he's not a great breeder and wasn't much of a runner. But maybe the owner of one of the infertile stallions wants to get at least some stud fees and have some live foals to point to."

"Or what if Dutton stole sperm from a really good breeder?"

"Yeah. Whose offspring do pretty well on the track. Couldn't be a famous racer, or a big well-known barn. So a modest racer who's bred some okay foals and has reasonable stud fees, so that this unexceptional infertile stallion begins to throw the occasional decent runner."

"So Dutton would be breaking all the Jockey Club rules about not doing artificial insemination with Thoroughbreds." Meg was staring at Michael with her hands clenched in her lap.

"Exactly. The owner of the infertile stud would have to be in on it, and whoever assisted at the stallion barn, and if Dutton brought a helper, he'd have to be part of it too. They'll often leave a mare at the stallion farms for a couple of days so there can be multiple coverings, and they'll rely on the stallion grooms there. Well, maybe the stud owner actually helps with the breeding, or his head groom helps to limit the numbers of folks who know what's going on."

"But—"

"He'd have to collect the fertile stallion's semen, put

his own recipe of a semen extender in it, and get it over to the farm with the sterile stud as quickly as possible. That's why there'd have to be a gap in his schedule before he went to that stallion's farm late in the day, or early evening."

"How could he steal the semen of a good stud without being seen?"

"It wouldn't be as hard as you'd think, not with a small farm. And there're plenty of folks who've made money at something else, who know next to nothing about horses but want to get into the racing game, and have more money than sense. So if you bribe one of their grooms, or you just say, 'I need a complete collection for additional sperm testing.' Or you pour what you collect from the stick-and-cup after the live breeding, the way you normally would to do the usual microscopic evaluation of the semen, but then you put it in a receptacle with your own extender, when nobody's looking, I mean, that's doable. Then you rush to the other farm where everyone's in cahoots."

Meg nodded, and then said, "But would there be enough money in it?"

"I don't know. I guess it depends on whether the only motive is money, or whether the owner of the stallion is trying to look like he's a knowledgeable horse- man who didn't buy a dud. But there're other possibil- ities too with other stallions we don't consider infertile."

"Like what?"

"What if you had a stallion that had a temporary condition and you didn't want anyone to know. A high fever that overheats the scrotum from a viral infection, or an injury that makes the horse lie down for too long, overheating the scrotum, those can cause permanent infertility, but it can also be temporary. Maybe the owner wants no question about his sterility and wants him breeding right through. He could use Dutton's stallion's sperm with no danger, and at least get a mare or two in foal while he waits for his horse to recover, thereby keeping from casting aspersions on his horse's performance. The horses I've been investigating don't fall into that category, but that could work. I can see a lot of ways you could do this if the stallion owners are as dishonest as Dutton.

"And there could be someone who owns a mare who wants to breed with a better stud than he can afford who's willing to say the dud is the sire if he can get sperm from a good stallion at a reduced rate." Michael shrugged and looked at her then, his lips drawn and his jaw tight.

"So how should we react? You know I could fire Dutton now, but it doesn't look to me as though we have any proof."

"No, we definitely don't. But I am trying to document all sorts of things I haven't mentioned. I'm going to the clinic late at night and running through all kinds of records to see what I can find. But there's actually a bigger philosophical question that I think's involved."

Michael dropped his fork on his empty plate and leaned back in his chair, his thick dark hair curling on his forehead, his blue eyes strained and hot looking. "Is it enough to find that Dutton's dishonest and just get rid of him for our own sakes? Or do we need to find the extent of his dishonesty and report him to the proper authorities so he loses his license, or is at least stopped from doing the crap he's doing here once he leaves us?"

"Ah. Yes, I'd rather drum him out of the business and keep him from doing more harm. *If* we can come up with enough real proof to convince the licensing authorities, or the Jockey Club at the very least."

"That groom up in Louisville that Jo told you about who never wants to work with us again. The fellow who's a cousin of the groom at Claiborne? I'm going to try to contact him too, and see what he has to say. Getting him to talk probably won't be all that easy, but it's definitely worth a shot."

Meg had finished her iced tea, and she slipped Jessie an ice cube, which she carried across to her bed. "I also think we need to find out something about Dutton's background. He was born and raised in Middleburg, Virginia, and if I remember right, his mother lives there still today. I've been thinking there may be a way to find out something about him before he came here."

"That'd be worth doing. The more we know, the more we'll see what's the right thing to do."

"But we surely don't want to stir up a lawsuit."

"No, we definitely don't! There's something else too." Michael told her about Dutton making the Millers pay their vet bills in one lump sum, and how he'd told the daughter he wouldn't let that happen.

"Absolutely not. There're plenty of other folks too who've paid over time, and I'm certainly not willing to let that change. I'll phone Dutton tomorrow and make sure that's clearly understood."

"Good. He'll know you heard it from me, but that can't be helped. Anyway, I've got to go. Thanks for dinner."

"You're welcome."

Meg waved to him as he pulled into the drive—and suddenly saw Michael again, Michael when he was little, two-and-a-half or maybe three, when they'd come down from Pennsylvania, where Cliff had worked then, to visit his family on their farm.

All the cousins were there, all of them older than Michael, and she'd gotten him up from a nap so he could have time to play. He'd been quiet and shy and unsure, looking worried to Meg, as though he'd rather be alone, or go straight back to bed.

And then they'd done what kids do, picking on the littlest one, keeping him from playing with them, hooping and hollering and running away from him, and hiding when he tried to find them, saying things to him Meg couldn't hear with malice on their mouths. Missy had seemed confused by the whole thing, not wanting to hurt her brother, but not knowing how to react. And then Michael had disappeared.

She'd found him on a step outside the kitchen door, looking tired and sad, with his elbows on his knees, and his dark curly head leaning on one hand. Meg had sat down and put her arm around him, and he'd looked up with his forehead crinkled and his eyes as old as the ages. "Why are they so mean?"

"I don't know, sweetie. It's the way folks are sometimes when they get together. It makes 'em feel good to pick on somebody. But us seeing how it feels can make us understand why we shouldn't do that to anybody else."

He'd looked at her as though that was no consolation, but he didn't say anything else. They'd sat there, with her rubbing his back, till Cliff came out to look for them.

You're gettin' old, Meg.

Seeing pieces of the past for no reason.

You'll be retelling tales folks have heard too often before you can shake a stick.

CHAPTER FIVE

Wednesday, April 21st, 1965

Jo had put Sam, her big chestnut gelding, in the cross-ties in the barn closest to Meg's cabin where her mare, and her friend Spencer's two horses, were stabled as well. She was standing close to the wide doorway a foot or so in front of Sam, looking out to the west across the riding area toward the deep woods, watching Ross play in the sandy soil close up to the door. He'd squatted in the dirt, and was pushing and pulling a small blue car, making noises that seemed to mean something to him, while shoving sand into little mounds.

He was sixteen months old, and he walked well, and talked just fine, and understood a whole lot, and didn't seem to have many more nightmares than any other small child, and Jo was thinking about what he'd gone through and how much worse it could've been, when Sam—who'd been standing still, ruffling his lips across the back of her shirt—jumped a foot straight up

in the air, then came right back down without touching
Jo anywhere, as Meg walked through the east door thirty
feet away.

"I'm sorry, Jo. I should've spoken before I got to the
door so I kept from startling Sam."

"He's fine. He was just off in his own little world and
didn't hear you on the drive. You sure you don't mind
watching Ross?"

"No. We'll have fun. You need to get out and ride."

"Would an hour be okay?"

"Certainly. Stay out as long as you'd like." Meg
walked along Sam's left side, patting him on her way past,
then stopped and stood beside Ross.

That was when Emmy, Jo's boxer-mutt, trotted into
the east end of the barn and walked past Sam and Jo,
wagging her whole rear end, before she sat down between
Meg and Ross, where she lifted her right front paw,
which Meg promptly shook. "I wish Jessie would behave
as well as Emmy does with the horses."

"Emmy showed up when she was two months old, so
she was easier to train. She got kicked once too, which
taught her what she needed to know without actually
hurting her much." Jo had already brushed Sam, and she
smoothed a saddle pad on his back, then settled her used
dressage saddle on top, and tightened the short girth.
"You know, Meg, I look at Ross, and I think about what
we went through last year, and how close he came to
being killed, and sometimes the relief of seeing him here,
as healthy as he is, is almost overwhelming."

"I can't imagine why it wouldn't be."

"He's more afraid of strange men than he was before. But even that's beginning to get better. And I think about you losing your daughter, and wonder how you stood it."

"You have no choice, when it happens. Missy was older too, and I expect that helped. She was about to graduate from William and Mary, so she'd had time to become something of what she wanted to be."

"Even so—"

"She was killed in a car accident that wasn't her fault, a good deal like your brother, Tommy. So it wasn't a deliberate assault like you faced with Ross."

"I didn't know what happened. I thought—"

"It was after Missy died that Cliff decided to start his own clinic, and I believe that helped. It gave us something outside ourselves to take on together. We worked, and prayed, and supported each other, and with time doing what it does to heal, it helped us go on. You'd get through it too, if it happened to you. It's either that, or you fall apart, and you and Alan wouldn't do that."

"I hope not. But you never know till you're faced with it."

"I suspect that's probably true." Meg had picked Ross up when he'd fallen on his face and was wiping sand off his mouth with a large white handkerchief she'd pulled from inside her sleeve.

Jo said, "We lost my daddy when I was young, and Mama with a brain tumor just before Tommy died. And I can see that getting to know Alan, with what he'd been through in the war, helped me start again."

"We don't get to be safe here. We can't avoid suffering. And it wouldn't be good for us if we did. We'd never look beyond what we can grasp for ourselves."

"True." Jo slid her stirrups to the bottom of the leathers and retightened the girth.

"Something I've been meaning to ask you. Do I remember you telling me that you have a friend whose mother came from Middleburg, Virginia?"

"Yeah, Spencer Franklin."

"He the one who lives in your tenant house?"

"Yep. You prob'ly haven't seen him much. He's started a new horse-trailer business, and he's hardly ever home."

"Does Spencer still have family in Middleburg?"

"I think there may be some cousins."

"Dutton Harris was born and raised in Middleburg, and I believe his mother lives there still today. And I wonder if you'd be willing to ask Spencer if he could find out something about Dutton Harris's background? Ross, don't put sand in your mouth. It's not something you can eat."

"You're still worried about Dutton?"

"More as time goes on."

"I'll ask Spencer to see what he can find out when he comes to feed his horses tonight."

"I believe we've got reason to think Dutton's truly unethical."

"Can't you fire him?"

"I could. But if he's as dishonest as we fear, I'd like to have evidence to lodge with the Jockey Club, and perhaps even the licensing authorities, to keep him from working as a vet."

"Ah." Sam was tacked up, and Jo had put on her helmet, and Meg picked Ross up and stepped out of the way so Jo could walk Sam out their end of the aisleway. "We'll go through the woods for a while, then do some work in the riding area."

"We'll stay here while Ross is having fun with his car, and then we'll walk to my house so he can play the piano. I haven't seen your Uncle Toss today."

"He's gone to talk to a client. They may want us to take a couple more mares who're already in foal."

Friday, April 23rd, 1965

It might've been the storm that woke her. Though she often woke in the night with her mind working and wandering from one thing to another. The last few weeks it'd been Dutton Harris—from how Cliff would've handled him, to what she ought to do, to how they could run the practice after he was gone.

Meg told herself to listen to the rain pounding on the cedar shakes while the wind worked at the windows—to close her eyes, and relax every muscle, while she pictured the world swirling in the dark, getting buffeted by the storm.

But then she started thinking about her sister, and how she'd died when she was twelve—and how her mother had gotten quiet. There were no more picnics and day trips. No more visits to parks and museums. But every Sunday afternoon was spent at Elaine's grave.

Elaine had been only eighteen months younger, and Meg had missed her in her bones and her blood. But when Meg had gotten to high school, she'd wanted to feel like she could join the choir and the orchestra and the debating club, and go on youth group outings with her brother, and feel like she was part of life again, looking toward the future. And she had—without her mother objecting. But there'd still been a shadow of guilt in her heart as she'd watched her mother day after day, doing her duty in all kinds of ways without a word of complaint.

Her mama had gotten so she'd laughed again, and gone to events on the post with Meg's daddy the way she had before. She'd kept on teaching her Sunday school class, and sewed for folks in the church, but she was always quieter than she'd been before Elaine died. She'd lost two daughters when they were babies, and Elaine's death was almost like a blow that broke open an old wound and kept it from closing again.

Meg wished she'd been able to help her more, but she hadn't understood until she'd lost Missy, and her mother and daddy were both gone then before she'd known what to say.

Meg made herself remember when they were younger, when they'd all laughed and talked around the table eating her mother's homemade cooking—her apple dumplings and peach cobbler, her buttermilk biscuits and fried chicken, her roasts that fell off the bone—that had made them smile their whole lives.

But two minutes later Meg was back at the business, trying to think what she should do. And she told herself to turn on the light and read till she fell asleep.

Dorothy L. Sayers didn't begin to help.

Neither did G. K. Chesterton.

And Meg found herself staring at the old stone fireplace that faced her four-poster bed.

You know you're going to look through it sometime. You might as well get to it now, because you're not going to go back to sleep without getting up and doing something.

She found Cliff's lap desk in one of the cardboard boxes sitting against the stone chimney on the west wall of the cabin's loft that stretched above the music room and her bedroom on the east.

She set it on Cliff's big mahogany desk and turned on his brass lamp, which made the lap desk's figured walnut glow a dark, rich, golden honey color in the wide wash of the light.

It was a left-to-right rectangle when it was fully closed, its brass key plate flush with the wood like the brass straps on either side, with its hinges hidden in the back. But when Meg picked up the top and opened it away from her, setting it down on Cliff's desk, the top became a long, slanted writing surface covered with black leather. The tops of both halves could be unlocked and raised, opening up the compartments underneath, the deeper one with a shallow false bottom where Cliff had put her earliest letters, with two from his oldest friend.

Meg slid her hand across the smooth old leather, remembering the years she'd watched Cliff work on it, usually at night, while she'd read, or played piano, or did paperwork from the clinic. She could see him again in his truck too, when she'd gone with him on his rounds, waiting at a barn for an owner, filling out patient reports, the desk open on his lap.

Then she saw him the day he'd died, the way he'd been found in his truck. Slumped over with his head on the window, the lap desk open under the steering wheel, a single sheet of clinic letterhead on the floor beside his pen.

She hadn't read what he'd written then. She'd folded the paper and slipped it in the desk, then closed it one last time to take home to his office.

The rain tore at the window in front of her and lightning flashed across the night, and Meg watched it strike a second time before she opened the lid of the lap desk and pulled out the note she'd never read.

It was handwritten in Cliff's wandering scrawl, addressed to Ridgeway Russell, their family and business attorney, whom they both thought of as a friend.

Meg looked away before she read more, asking herself why Cliff would've written him. And why, for the hundredth time, she hadn't read it right away when she'd found it by his body.

You were crushed right then. But I expect it was more than that. I believe you were truly afraid that whatever it was Cliff had been writing had to do with what caused his death.

I think you simply didn't want to know if something horrible happened that'd brought on a heart attack. Or an embolism. Or perhaps a stroke. Whatever it was that killed him. You wanted him to slip away in some sort of peace and comfort. Not die with anger, or fear, or anxiety tearing away his life.

And yet you know that's nothing like you. From the day you were born, you've wanted to know rather than not know, ninety-nine times in a hundred, even if the truth hurts, and the news couldn't be worse.

The time has come to pick up that letter and do what you should've done then.

January 19, 1964
Dear Ridge,

If I'd known then what I found out today I never would have entered into an agreement with Dutton Harris. He is not a man of honor or honesty, and I intend to terminate our agreement as soon as I

There was a splotch of black ink next to the "I," a splash from Cliff's old fountain pen, and Meg touched it with her index finger, while tears gathered in her eyes.

I can't understand what could've happened after we talked at breakfast. Who could Cliff have spoken to?

Or what could've come to his notice?

Something unusual had to have happened, and I need to find out what that was as soon as I possibly can.

His appointment calendar might tell you something. It was there in the truck when he died. So it must be in with the rest of his things in one of the cardboard boxes.

She looked at them on the other side of the loft and stretched her arms out to the side. It was close to three, and she was getting tired, and she told herself to look for it in the morning. To call the clinic and get Sara to check the office calendar too, and see if something unexpected had been scheduled there.

Now she'd sit and read it once more. She'd touch the paper Cliff had touched. She'd remember him the way he'd been—smiling and smart, quiet and kind, dedicated to doing everything he did as well as anyone could, furious when he came across work that was sloppy or lazily done.

Meg went through the boxes first thing in the morning, Jessie stretched out beside her feet, where she sat and sorted through every single box after setting them up on Cliff's desk.

When she'd finished all eight, she still hadn't found it. And yet she knew she wouldn't have thrown it out, and she told herself to search through again, after she'd phoned the clinic.

She talked to Sara Fletcher, the office manager she'd trained, and told her she was trying to discover Cliff's schedule on the day he died, January 19, 1964, and would Sara please look through the appointment book while she waited on the line.

Sara read her Cliff's schedule for that whole day, and
Meg wrote it all down—the surgeries he'd done in the
clinic, the three farm visits in the afternoon, the hour-
and-a-half gap left at lunch, when he'd canceled a scheduled farm call.

They both knew that was highly unusual. Cliff rarely
took time for lunch. He carried fruit and cheese and
crackers, and ate wherever he was.

Meg thanked her and was ready to hang up, when
Sara said, "There is something else I remember that
seemed kinda unusual too. I prob'ly remember especially
'cause that was the day he died, but there was a woman
who called first thing that morning. I was gettin' settled
in right at seven, and Dr. Cliff was fixin' to scrub for
surgery, and I passed on the call to him. She asked for
him by name and said it'd only take a minute.

"He talked to her, right here in reception, and then
he told me to cancel that farm call and reschedule it the
next day. I b'lieve he agreed to meet her somewhere,
though I could tell from his side of the conversation that
he had no idea who she was. It sounded like she said
something that surprised him and persuaded him to see
her."

Sara sounded awkward when she said it, as though
that could be upsetting to Meg, but Meg just thanked her
and hung up and stared back at the row of boxes she'd
have to go through again.

She found Cliff's appointment book two hours later,

having gone through every box at least twice. It was stuck inside a cardboard file, full of notes he'd taken at a conference, that had been closed completely with a fold-over flap and two elastic bands. How it got there Meg couldn't imagine, but she'd packed up everything really quickly with a fraction of her mind on the job.

She opened it up with her ribs tight and her breath coming fast, her face hot and her eyes strained, and turned to the day that Cliff died, afraid of what she'd find.

He'd crossed off a routine appointment at a barn outside Versailles, and written in, "Midway. Lunch. Mrs. Anna Madden."

Meg reread the name that meant nothing to her, and tried to decide what to do first to find out how to reach her.

The library made the most sense, with telephone books from all over.

There were no Maddens in Versailles or Midway, either one. There were six in Lexington who weren't connected to the woman she wanted, and three dead ends in Georgetown. There weren't any in Frankfurt.

But there were two Maddens in Louisville—one answered, but wasn't Anna. The last phone rang without being answered till Meg finally hung up.

She told herself to play the piano, Chopin preludes to calm herself down, and take Jessie out for a walk, then call again after five.

Saturday, April 24th, 1965

Meg met Anna Madden at noon in Midway in a ma-and-pa diner in the middle of the one-block business district on the south side of the tracks.

She was short and thin and wore her sandy hair cropped close against her bones. She used very little make-up and wore no-nonsense clothes, and she lit a filtered Winston as soon as she sat down, even before she ordered coffee and a grilled-cheese sandwich.

She seemed to be considering Meg while they'd ordered and made small talk, but when Meg told her she'd been surprised to learn that Cliff had met her, she looked as though hearing that had freed her—that there were things she'd come there to say to Meg she was aching to get out.

"I called your husband and asked to meet him because I had important information I presumed he'd want to hear. I certainly would've if I'd had Dutton Harris working for me. I'd want to know what kind of man I'd hired, that I never would've learned from him." Anna stubbed out her cigarette and drank her coffee as though she needed to do something with her hands before she said another word.

"My husband died a month before you folks hired Harris, and it wasn't until that next January, when I got in touch with your husband, that I'd come to the place where I figured it was the only thing left I could do. And then with him dyin' like he did, it didn't do a licka good. I don't mean any disrespect. I admired your husband right off, and I know if he'd lived he'd have taken some action."

"I know he was trying to. He was writing a letter to his lawyer about Dutton right when he died. That was the letter I told you I didn't read until yesterday."

"Did you know that the veterinary clinic Harris worked for in Louisville was a large- and a small-animal practice?" She was brushing ash off her khaki pants and the front of her white linen blouse.

"I remember that, yes."

"My husband, Phillip, worked there as well. There were three other vets in the practice, and everyone did everything, though some had their preferences, just like you'd expect. Harris preferred the equine practice to the cattle and small animals, and my husband preferred the dogs and cats, and was endeavoring to specialize in small-animal surgery."

Anna Madden pushed the plate with her half-eaten grilled cheese off to one side and lit another Winston. Her small brown eyes were half hidden by her eyebrows, pulled together, creasing her forehead, while she tapped two fingers on the table. "My husband was a fine veterinarian, but he was also an unusually sensitive person. He was one of life's natural worriers, and he rethought every action he took. He stayed up nights fretting about our children. And he always took the traumas to heart with the animals he worked on, especially if he particularly liked the folks they belonged to."

Meg nodded, as she cut up her salad. "My husband became attached to his horses too, and he never could just slough it off when they didn't do well. He worked with small animals in the early years too, and I think in some ways that can be even more personal—at least it was for Cliff."

"It was for Phillip too. Anyway, it was 1963, early in February, that my husband's mother died very unexpectedly. Phillip was terribly upset, even more than I would've expected. After the wake, when we'd all gotten home, he had two or three drinks on his own. He normally hardly drank at all. Nothing all week till Friday and Saturday, and then just a bottle of beer, or maybe a glass of wine. But the day his mother was buried, it seemed like he was trying to blot it out of his mind on purpose. Like he wanted to drift off to sleep and wake up another day.

"And then he got a call about eight o'clock from the colleague at the clinic who was on call that night. He was very ill with a high fever and a really bad case of stomach flu, and he couldn't go in to work. The trouble was there was a young Labrador who'd been in labor for hours and appeared to need a cesarean, at least based on the phone conversation he'd had with her owners, who should've called hours earlier but didn't out of ignorance.

"Phillip, being conscientious like he was, insisted on going in, since nobody else was available. And he went ahead and performed the cesarean on a very complicated case. There was a dead puppy stuck right where the Y-shaped birth canal comes together, and the mother and all but one of the puppies ended up dying before it was through.

"He'd had to do surgery without an assistant, with the owners waiting in the lobby, which increased the pressure too. And then, Dutton Harris came in to do something, I'm not sure what, and saw Phillip closing up after the operation.

"Phillip was in tears, and Dutton could tell he'd been drinking. So Dutton took the live puppy out to the dog's owners and explained what had happened, and covered for Phillip being halfway drunk. It would've been a very difficult surgery even if Phillip hadn't had a single drink. The poor dog had been in labor so long there'd been internal tearing, and three puppies were dead when he opened her up, but Phillip was beside himself, blaming himself for it all, when from what he admitted later, it probably wouldn't have been any different if he'd been stone-cold sober.

"But Dutton saw it as an opportunity, and he started blackmailing Phillip that February of 1963. Phillip didn't tell me about the blackmail till that August. Though I knew very well that something was wrong. He was getting to be more and more depressed, and a whole lot more anxious, but I didn't know why, other than that surgery he'd been blaming himself for since."

"That must've been terrible for both of you."

"It was. And Dutton must've made his days a misery, needling him whenever they met in whatever way he could. But Phillip told me nothing about it. He took cash out of the bank every month and gave it to Dutton, with me completely in the dark. He paid the bills and balanced the checkbook, and all I knew was he was more concerned about money than normal. I manage a doctor's office in Louisville, and I ran the house and cared for the children, while he oversaw our finances and did maintenance on the house."

Anna Madden lit another cigarette using the end of the last, and swallowed the rest of her coffee. "On August 12th, 1963, Phillip told me Dutton was blackmailing him. That he threatened him with telling the dog's owners Phillip had been incapable of performing the surgery and was totally responsible for the loss of the dogs, which could've led to a lawsuit. He said he'd report him to the licensing authorities and make sure he lost his license. And Phillip was beside himself so that nothin' I said seemed to help. I told him we should talk to a lawyer, and report Dutton to the police, but, of course, there was no evidence of blackmail, with only the cash payments. Phillip seemed a little calmer by the time we went to bed, and then in the morning he called me at work and asked me to meet him at home for lunch, when he sounded more like himself. Just goes to show you how little I understood."

Anna Madden stubbed out her cigarette and stared at her hands as though she had to steel herself to say anything more.

Meg watched, and drank her iced tea, and knew in her bones that she shouldn't say a word, but let Anna take her time.

"When I drove in the driveway, Phillip's truck was there, and he was sitting behind the wheel, his head back against the seat, his eyes closed tight. He'd injected himself with dog anesthetic, and he'd prob'ly been dead an hour."

Meg said, "I'm so sorry."

And Anna glanced at Meg and nodded—when they both knew no words could help. "The neighbors came out and stood around and stared when they saw the police and the ambulance. And then the children came home as they were taking him away, and I had to find a way to tell them what their dad had done."

The waitress came, and Meg asked for the check so they'd be left alone.

"It wasn't till the next day that I called Dutton and told him what I thought of him. And all he said was 'Phillip was a weakling. He shouldn't have been a vet.'"

"I can almost hear Dutton saying it."

"I talked to my lawyer, hoping there was a way to prosecute Harris, but there wasn't anything he could see to do. Phillip told me what had happened, but he didn't write a note, and even if he had, there was no way to prove Harris had demanded money."

"And then in September, Harris left and came to us in Lexington."

"Yes." Anna played with her lighter, twirling it on the table, before she lit another smoke. "The next few months all I could manage was to get food on the table, and pay the bills, and try to help our children cope with Phillip's death. They were eight and six then, and completely confused and crushed. And then in January of 1964, I began to look past our daily troubles, and decided the only action I could take was to tell your husband what Dutton Harris had done."

"And then he died without talking to me, so I didn't know what to do."

"Do you think our conversation led to his heart attack? If it was a heart attack. It must've been something quick and unexpected. He seemed fine when I saw him, and the obituary didn't say."

"It was probably a heart attack. Though it could've been an aneurism, or maybe even a stroke. We didn't do an autopsy. I didn't see the point."

"I hope it wasn't because of me."

"No, it's not your fault at all."

They both sat in silence, lost in their own concerns, before Meg finished her tea and told Anna about Cliff's letter. "He intended to fire Dutton right away, and I know he would've told him why, as well as how disgusted he was. Cliff never would've put up with Dutton, not another hour."

"And what will you do now? Now that you know?"

"Could you send me a copy of your bank statements, showing those cash withdrawals for all those months? And write me a letter putting down everything that happened?"

Anna Madden thought about that. She looked as though she'd been caught her off guard and didn't know what to say.

"I know that might be a great deal to ask, since I'm virtually a perfect stranger, but—"

"If I block out the unrelated items, then yes, I guess, I

could send on the bank statements. The cash withdrawals are consistent, though that's not enough to prosecute Harris."

"No, but it's some kind of indication. There are other things he's doing now that are looking under-handed. And my son and I are trying to amass enough concrete evidence to limit his role in the profession. I can't say anything else. Not right at the moment."

"If I can help you in any way, I will."

"Thank you. I'll let you know what we decide to do."

CHAPTER SIX

Saturday, April 24th, 1965

Ronnie Holmes had gotten to the clinic at six that morning to read bacterial cultures Michael and Jerry were waiting on, and also get a head start on sorting the supply room that served the operating room. He intended to change the air filters in the air-conditioning system before he left too, and replace a fluorescent tube in the overhead lights in reception.

He wasn't scheduled to work that Saturday, but he could get a lot done fast when he came in early, and he was drinking coffee and humming to himself while examining sensitivity tests in ten incubated petri dishes, when he heard the door to employee parking open at the end of the hall.

He listened to the footsteps hitting the linoleum, and said, "Crap," quietly under his breath, when he recognized Dutton's walk. He stopped humming, but kept making the notes he'd copy later into patient files.

Ronnie knew Dutton was in the doorway behind him. He could feel him standing there, watching as he went about his work, raising the hair on his neck.

"Do I remember that you're married, Ronnie?"

"Yep."

"And you have a young child?"

"I have three. Eight, and four, and one-and-a-half."

"And am I correct in thinking you've been trained here to perform tasks for which you haven't been formally educated?"

"I have. Dr. MacInnes taught me how to do a fairly wide range of laboratory tests, and oversee supplies as well. I was a medic in Korea and got some extra training there too. And, of course, Dr. MacInnes knew I was kinda mechanical, and he sent me to get trained in our medical equipment."

"Though none of that training would necessarily transfer to another job."

"I don't rightly know." Ronnie pushed his glasses up his long knobby nose, and brushed his hair off his narrow forehead, his ordinary, forgettable face already looking uneasy.

"And you've been acquainted with the MacInneses for quite a while."

"Michael and I went to grade school together. He was two years behind, but I spent a lotta time at his house."

"Which I presume accounts for the special treatment you've received from the family."

"I don't know that it's been special treatment. The MacInneses have trained alotta folks. They've been real good to me, but I've always tried to go above-and-beyond in return."

"And I'd be correct in assuming you don't wish to lose this position?"

"Yes."

"Because I don't imagine finding another as congenial would be particularly easy."

Ronnie didn't answer. He stared at Harris and waited, his face hot and his chest tight, his breathing turning shallow.

"In case you haven't noticed, Clifford MacInnes isn't here anymore." There was a silence then between them while Ronnie swallowed and Dutton Harris watched. "You work for *me*, not the family. And yet there've been indications that information about our business, our medical supplies in particular, has passed from you to Meg MacInnes. Through Michael perhaps, or directly, which route I neither know nor care. What I can say with certainty is it's in your best interest to keep that from happening again." Dutton had taken off his beige linen sport jacket and draped it across one shoulder, as he stared straight at Ronnie Holmes with ice in his half-closed eyes. "Do I make myself clear? Otherwise there will be consequences you will have reason to regret."

"You couldn't've made yourself any clearer." Ronnie stared back, his lab stool swiveled toward Dutton, his hands in his lab coated lap, his face as neutral as he could make it with the anger in his blood.

Michael MacInnes had been on call during the night and he hadn't gotten home from a colic that actually turned out well till a little past four. He'd slept till eight, which was late for the horses, and he'd gone out to feed and water them, with Wolf right on his heels, before he came in and made breakfast.

He'd spent a lot of time in the last few days trying to get in touch with the groom he'd heard about through Jo who never wanted to work with MacInnes Equine again. Michael had talked to Buddy Jones, who'd told Jo about it to begin with, who'd been told by his friend, Charlie Smalls, what that other groom had said. He was Charlie's cousin, as it turned out, and there was much toing and froing, from what Michael was able to tell, and he still didn't know whether he'd ever be able to talk to the guy and find out what had happened.

He'd been going through his dad's infertility work too, cross-referencing with Dutton's records, and the more he read and put things together, the more he was convinced that Dutton was involved in something under-handed with at least three barns between Lexington and Louisville where stallions that were permanently infertile now appeared to be breeding foals.

But he told himself he needed a break, while he made toast and scrambled two eggs. He hadn't spent enough time with Laura, or ridden Drummond the way he should, and he needed to do it today. He called Laura and asked if she could come for lunch and spend the rest of the day, maybe taking a picnic and walking the fields, then going out to dinner and a film. She said she couldn't get there till one, but the rest of the day was free.

Michael put Carrick and Drummond in their paddocks and went to work stripping the stalls, forking manure and dirty straw into his old manure spreader. He was about to drive it out of the barn to spread the manure on his neighbor's back field—when the phone rang in the tack room.

It was Buddy Jones, Jo's friend, calling to tell him that the Louisville groom had agreed to talk to Michael that morning if he could get to his cousin's house in Frog Town by eleven. Buddy thought he was dreading it still, ready to run and not talk, and it was Charlie Smalls prompting him that had gotten him to the point of agreeing to actually meet at Charlie's sister Esther's house, not too far outside Versailles.

Michael wrote the address on the tack room blackboard and called Laura to ask her to wait if he got back late.

Esther Wilkes' house was a small white-clapboard cottage on the top of a low hill, south a couple miles off the Lexington Road, tucked back into hills and hollows with a few distantly scattered houses, most in poor repair.

Hers was painted and mowed around, with flowers growing by the wide roofed porch and a vegetable garden just visible past one corner of the back. Charlie Smalls was waiting for Michael on the front porch, wearing his khaki Claiborne uniform, sitting in a rush-seated chair, watching him climb the yard toward the house.

He said, "Dr. MacInnes," as he stood up and motioned Michael to the chair beside his. "I'm Charlie Smalls." He was thin and dark-skinned with a few threads of gray in his close-cropped hair, his face unlined, though he must've been sixty, every bit of him strong looking from years of working with horses.

"Thank you for arranging for me to meet your cousin. I really need to understand what our people are doing wrong."

"It's gonna be real hard for Tate. Talkin' behind the wrong back could lose him his job."

"I won't tell anyone else what he says without his okay."

"That's what Buddy told me, and I do b'lieve it's the only reason Tate decided to come. I'll step in and tell him you're here."

Charlie wasn't tall, maybe five eight or nine, but Tate Smalls was short, five four and wiry, fit and quick like a jockey. He was younger than Charlie too, maybe in his forties, and his eyes were looking everywhere except at Michael as he sat in the chair that faced him.

Michael smiled and introduced himself, then said, "I really appreciate you agreeing to meet me. I expect something must've happened that gave you a very poor picture of MacInnes Equine, and that's not how my mom and I want to do business. She and my dad tried really hard to do everything honestly and aboveboard and take excellent care of every horse he treated, and that's the way we want to keep on. But if we don't know what's going on, we won't be able to fix it."

Tate Smalls nodded, but didn't say anything. He just tapped one low-heeled cowboy boot on the unpainted floor and gripped the arms of his chair.

"So. I figure it must've been something one of our vets did."

"I gotta have your word you won't tell nobody else."

"My mother still owns the practice, and it'll be her decision what we do to fix whatever's been done wrong, so I pretty much have to tell her."

"Ain't no way to fix it. Ya cain't bring back the dead."

"Ah." Michael paused and looked at the floor before he tried again. "So would it be alright for me to tell her, as long as she agrees not to tell anyone else?"

"You're asking me to trust you more than I got reason to."

"That's true. You don't know me. But I bet you knew my dad."

"I did. He was a man of his word."

"He was. And my mom and I want the clinic to be run the way he ran it and honor his name."

Tate didn't say anything else. He was chewing gum and he took it out and wrapped it in its wrapper and laid it on the table between his chair and Charlie's.

Charlie said, "You gonna talk to him or not? Ya got him out here like you would. Once ya tell him, he'll see why it ain't so easy."

Nobody said anything for more than a minute. Michael sat with his hands on his thighs, trying not to stare at Tate. Tate gazed beyond Michael down the hill toward the gravel road—till he looked straight at him once and then began to talk.

"Up till five weeks ago I worked for Golden Window Farm as a stallion groom, and one of the stallions I looked after was a big bay called Night Captain. He run pretty good on the track, and he'd been at stud for six years, and the owner of the farm, he decided to send him down to Florida last month so he could breed down there for mosta the season. His foals ain't been nothing special. They ain't running good, and his stud fee was slippin', and I reckon they figured he might could do better down there in Ocala where the competition ain't so stiff."

Michael filled in the silence that followed with, "I know other folks who've done that."

"We was flying him to Florida, with a two-year-old colt who'd been sold to a barn down there, and I was taking them on the flight. You know how they set up a freight plane, with movable stalls and all, and other freight stowed around. We bring the straw bedding, and the water, and the hay they're used to, and we try to get 'em settled down so there won't be no trouble in the air. We set bales of straw too, like you might expect, between them and the wall of the plane so they won't do no damage if they was to kick out."

"Right." Michael nodded and slid his hands toward his knees.

"Well, your Dr. Harris, he was going too, and some assistant whose name I don't know, and it seemed kinda

peculiar right from the start. Captain'd never give me no
trouble, and the two-year-old was a good little guy, so it
wasn't nothing I couldn't handle on my own like normal.
But there they were, and we took off and got going, and
I fed and watered the boys, and I sat down on a bale of
straw and leaned back against the side of the plane. I'd
brought me a horse-care magazine, and I was startin' in,
while Harris and the other guy went up front where
there was a couple seats in the cabin.

"Then the other guy come back with a plastic cup of
coffee and asked if I'd like some, and I thanked him and
took it. He went back, and I flipped through the magazine and drank some of the coffee, that turned out to be
real bitter, and I got to feelin' kind of woozy. It seemed
real strange to feel that way, and I reckoned it had something to do with the coffee I was drinkin'. And I poured
it out in a thermos I'd brought, where I'd drunk most of
the water, and I sat back down, and leaned against the
wall, and shut my eyes for a minute.

"Well, it wasn't long till Harris and the other guy
come back to where I was and looked to see if the coffee
was gone. I figured by then something funny was going
on, and I kept my eyes shut and let 'em think I was
sleepin'. That's when Harris, standin' there with his back
to me, musta pulled out a loaded syringe, and he went
right ahead and put Night Captain down. Cap had just
been standing there, just normal, just bracing his legs and
chewin' some hay, and that son of a bitch put him down
before I could see it comin'. Captain went down hard on
the floor, and it panicked the two-year-old, and I got up

and went to quietin' him, and the guy with Harris grabbed me by the throat and knocked me up against the wall of the plane.

"Harris told me that if I said a word, I'd never work in Kentucky again, and a whole lot of nasty things would happen to my family. He said they'd be saying that Captain had gone berserk and had to be put down, and I was gonna agree with that and keep my mouth shut."

Michael was half out of his chair, staring hard at Tate. "That's criminal! Harris oughtta be—"

"Yep. I figured the owner musta set it up to get him the insurance. I know Captain was real well insured, and having a vet there to testify would give weight to making his case."

"I don't know what to say. I don't."

"When I got back to Lexington, I up and quit my job that day, and the owner he threatened me too, beatin' around the bush more, but making the same point. I found me a job at a small barn in Louisville, and I swear to God I never want to see any one of them three again, not as long as I live."

"That's worse than I imagined it ever could've been. Was the other guy's name Webber Swede?"

"I reckon that sounds pretty close."

"I'll tell you this, Harris has done other dishonest things too, and we're trying to get enough evidence that we can make him lose his license, and this might help that happen. You might have to testify, though. And maybe write it down. And I know that's asking a lot."

Tate Smalls looked at Michael without saying anything while he unwrapped another stick of gum, and then he shook his head. "No, sir, I won't. I don't trust Harris, or that other jaybird who was with him, not to do what they say and go and hurt my family. I'm a Negro man trying to make a livin', and I ain't free to do everything I might like if things was different. I'm asking you to understand, and go on and act accordingly."

Michael looked at Charlie too, and Esther Wilkes as she came out her front door, and crossed her arms across her middle, her broad black face set and serious, her eyes fixed on his. Michael nodded, and waited awhile before he spoke. "I understand. And I don't blame you. I won't say anything about this except to my mother, like we agreed. But believe me, we'll do everything we can to stop Harris from ever hurting a horse again."

Sunday, April 25th, 1965

Jo and Emmy walked over, listening to mares and babies cropping grass, watching them watch them, as they walked past in the gathering dark. The moon was up throwing shadows, and with the scent of the fields and the breeze on her face, Jo listened to her boots on gravel and was glad to be right where she was on a day when everyone she loved was safe.

She'd phoned ahead, so Meg was expecting her, and she opened the door and walked in the way Meg did at her house.

Jessie was there waiting for Emmy and the two of

them wagged and sniffed every body part, while Jo walked through the kitchen to the living room in the back.

"So Ross is in bed?" Meg had taken off her reading glasses and was setting her book on the arm of her chair.

"He's sound asleep. And Alan's actually taking time to sit and read a novel."

"Good for him. Hot chocolate? Or iced tea?"

"Maybe just a glass of water."

They sat in the high-backed, white-linen chairs on either side of the fireplace, the dogs lying on the rug in between —Meg, with a pad of unlined paper in her lap, watching Jo settle in. "I want to take notes on whatever you've learned."

"It's just what Spencer heard from his cousin, so it's all anecdotal."

Meg smiled and said, "That's what I expected."

"She did interview a bunch of other people, 'cause with Dutton's mother having lived there for years, there're plenty of folks who know about the family, or at least have an opinion."

"Middleburg's a small town, and country folks pay attention."

"Exactly."

"And that can be good or bad, depending on where you're sitting." Meg smiled at Jo, then leaned down and rubbed Emmy's shoulder.

"Right. I brought notes, but I doubt I'm going to

need them. Gossip's easy to remember. Tell Emmy to go lie down if she's begging for too much attention."

"No, she's doin' just fine."

"So it seems like Dutton's mother and daddy bought a house there in Middleburg just after Dutton was born. It was a nice old house with a lotta land, and his mother always had horses. She rode with the hunt, and Dutton rode too, starting with ponies when he was little, but it didn't seem like he enjoyed it much. Didn't seem to care about the horses the way his mother did."

"*I* don't think he cares a lick about any of them now."

"His father was a lawyer in Washington DC, a Federal Trade Commission lawyer some time or other, and was a big supporter of Franklin Roosevelt. He might've had a political appointment during the war too, but the cousin wasn't sure. Seems like he was a very attractive man, and Dutton's mother was good looking too, though she was a quiet sort of person who was active in a couple of charities, but always stayed in Middleburg, riding her horses and doting on Dutton, while the dad lived most weeks in Washington and showed up on the weekends."

"Did folks think they were close?" Meg smoothed her hair toward her chignon and sipped her iced tea.

"Not from what I could tell. Rumor has it that he'd married her for her connections. Her daddy'd been a doctor from an old important Massachusetts family that lost most of what it'd had during the Depression, but was still well liked and respected."

"What do they say about Dutton's side?"

"Dutton's dad came from some Connecticut family

that went to Yale for generations, but ended up losing its money, through drunkenness and laziness supposedly. So they reckon he looked around to marry more, and I guess Dutton's mom had some of her own from her mother's relations. Folks thought Dutton's dad wanted a wife who could be a good hostess and help him make social contacts, but other than that, he didn't pay much attention."

"Not the kind of husband anyone I know would want."

"No. They do say Dutton's father was a very charismatic, charming sort of guy, and folks think he had affairs when he was in Washington, which the mother seemed to put up with. She didn't look to be wildly impressed by him. But everybody says she was obsessed with Dutton. That that's where her whole life was centered, though the father seemed to be generally critical and belittle him in front of folks. *She* thought Dutton could do no wrong. His dad thought he couldn't do a single thing right."

"That can make it difficult to raise up a child." Meg turned over a new page, after writing one last note.

"Anyway, Dutton went to the University of Virginia, when he didn't get into Yale. His mother's father wanted him to be a doctor, but he told somebody he couldn't stand the thought of taking care of fat, boring, commonplace people with colds and cancer, and having to learn to cater to them."

"Ah. Regular folks like us."

"Yes. His dad thought he wasn't smart enough to become a lawyer. But then Dutton never seemed to study. He took a horse to UV too, and mostly played around. Though some say there was a professor there who suggested he become a vet, since he had all the connections in Virginia among the monied horsey set to make a successful career. Whether that carried weight or not, by the time he graduated he'd managed to pull his grades up. Nobody in Middleburg thought he was dumb like his dad did. They thought he was plenty smart, but not a very nice guy."

"Sounds like they knew him pretty well."

"'Course, whatever plans he had, World War II intervened. He was twenty-two in 1942, and rumor has it Dutton's mother pressured his father into getting Dutton a desk job in Washington, somewhere in the military, by calling in favors from Roosevelt. When Truman took over, some of the father's influence disappeared, and then the father was caught in some sort of illegal deal and lost his job with the law firm. Someone who knew Dutton in Washington said the fact that his dad did something illegal didn't seem to bother Dutton. It was more that he got caught. Dutton used to say, 'Everyone's out for number one. The ones who say they aren't are either lying, or flat out bone-deep dumb."

Meg said, "That's the Dutton I know. Though he sure said the opposite when we interviewed him for the job."

"After the dad lost his job, Dutton's parents separated for good, though they never did divorce. The father did some consulting work in DC, and then he died suddenly, right when Dutton's mom sold the farm. She bought something small, and kept a horse at a friend's house, and

still rides at sixty-five. She took a job as a receptionist/
secretary at The Chronicle there in Middleburg, which is
now called *The Chronicle Of The Horse*, and works there
today. She had a degree in English literature but hadn't
worked before, except for various charities.

"Anyway, after the war Dutton got his vet degree at
UK, and then joined a clinic in Middleburg, which made
Mama very happy. Folks say he didn't feel properly
appreciated there, and didn't get along with some of the
older vets in the practice, and he took the job in Louisville in 1956." Jo took the clip off her ponytail and let
her hair hang loose on her shoulders as though she was
tired of it being held tight.

Then Meg set her pen down and drank the last of her
tea. "Dutton's mother calls him at the clinic occasionally,
and yet he rarely agrees to speak to her. The receptionists
can hear that that hurts her, and they also think they hear
contempt in his voice when he talks about her."

"Apparently he's always treated her like she's some
kind of burden he has to bear."

"I've seen that happen before to mothers who dote
on one child or another. Especially an only child."

"So is any of that a help?" Jo had finished her glass of
water and was rubbing Emmy's chin.

"Yes, it surely is. It doesn't give me a great deal of
insight into what to do about him, but I do believe it
helps me understand what kind of person he is."

"They also said he has affairs like his dad. Usually
with married women who can't expect marriage, and he's

left a lot of heartache in his wake. At least he did in Middleburg."

"He never speaks about his private life, but he does still go to Louisville a great deal, and belongs to some fancy club there. There have been women who phone the clinic, but he rarely takes a call. Have you talked to Buddy Jones, by any chance?"

"No. Not in a couple of weeks. Why?"

"He arranged for Michael to talk to the groom who'd said he didn't want to work with MacInnes Equine again. I'm not at liberty to say more, but he's confirmed that Dutton has performed appalling and despicable acts, apparently just for the money. Something's got to be done, Jo, and I sure wish I knew what."

CHAPTER SEVEN

Tuesday, April 27th, 1965

Michael drove to Frank Sperry's after his last call of the afternoon, east on the Old Frankfort Pike where it cuts across the Midway Road between Versailles and Midway, then south onto Elkchester Road, with its quick turns and twists, that took him to Frank's place on a one-lane road he couldn't begin to name that led to Rice further on.

Frank had seventy acres in hay and tobacco, a small house, an old tobacco barn, and a four-stall barn where he kept two horses he no longer rode but couldn't bear to part with.

He was in his late sixties, and had spent his life as a breeding manager for a middle-sized farm where the people who'd cared about the breeding and racing had grown old and died off, and their kids had wanted a life up east with nothing to do with horses.

Frank had retired a few months before and taken up

his own life, with his wife still working beside him, his kids long grown but staying in the Bluegrass with his grandkids, who came for the horses, and the stories, and their grandmother's biscuits, plus something smooth and quiet and slow that seemed to soothe their souls.

He'd been a good friend to Michael's folks, and one of the long-time horsemen his dad had seen good reason to consult. For there wasn't much Frank didn't know about Thoroughbred breeding and racing in Kentucky, and Michael came to probe and pick and see what he could learn.

After they'd talked about Cliff, and Meg, and the days they'd done things together, and about Jo's Uncle Toss and their monthly penny poker night, Frank rolled a cigarette, sitting on his porch step, watching his geldings in their paddock, before he slid his sunglasses down to the end of his nose and looked Michael in the eye. "Now that we got that outta the way, tell me what's on your mind."

"Watcher. What do you know about him?"

"Now, *there* is a smart horse. Ornery as hell. Don't know if he got overhauled real bad by some fool when he was a baby, but he's never wanted to do what any of us humans have in mind since the day I first saw him."

"You've known him a long time?"

"Yep. He was bred down the road. Small farm. Bred and foaled by Gary Sykes. He comes outta War Admiral's line, and they say Gary won a chance to breed his mare to Watcher's sire in some kinda all-night card game. Unlikely he'd of gotten that booking any other way. His mare was nothin' to write home about, and wouldn't't've been acceptable to the sire's owner otherwise."

"I never heard a word about a card game, even from my dad."

"Don't know that many have."

"Yeah, that probably makes sense."

"I will say Watcher's sure somethin' to look at. Coal black. White stripe on his nose. Confirmation that don't quit. Disposition you don't wantta meet. Mean, even. More than ornery. Nobody thought much of his chances on the track, 'cause he hated to train, and run too. My old boss, Greg Grayson, bought him as a yearling and give 'em a real good trainer. Dead now, Artie is. But he did his best with Watcher. Tried to figure out how to get through to him, 'cause he's real athletic, real coordinated, fast as can be, and he shoulda run good.

"He didn't do squat as a two-year-old, but Artie got him goin' as a three-year-old, and he won four or five real decent races, surprisin' Artie as much as anybody— and then he upped and stopped runnin'. *Refused* to train. *Refused* to run. Nobody could make him do what he didn't want to do. They'd take him out near a track and he'd dig in and throw a fit, and get real dangerous. So Greg decided to put him to stud. He had 'specially good breeding on his sire's side, like I said—but he didn't wanta breed neither."

"That's what Dad said in his notes."

"Your dad, he got nineteen or twenty mares in foal the first year, but it was real touch and go. Watcher don't like mares. He don't. I mean it looked for a while like he got kinda interested in three or four nice little chestnuts, but that didn't last. He just flat out refused to breed, and it got real dangerous, to him and the mares, and the rest of us around him.

"I don't talk about it when there're ladies present, but he'd masturbate all the time. Even with them ring things to keep him from doing it. He would, you know how they do, rather than have anything to do with some mare. I think he decided he was never goin' to do anything anybody wanted him to do ever again. Then your dad was gone, and he was the only one who had any luck at all with Watcher. And his owner was ready to put him down, for lack of any other ideas, when the guy over to Golden Window Farm, he up and bought him sometime last fall. Paid next to nothin' for him, but I heard it's been just the same. Watcher don't cooperate."

"What would you say if I told you he's gotten four mares in foal this spring?"

"I wouldn't believe it, less I saw him do it with my own eyes."

"That's what Dutton Harris is claiming since he's been working with Watcher."

"Shoot. If your dad give up on him, I ain't countin' on Dutton Harris, I can tell ya that."

"Can I count on you not to say anything about what I'm going to tell you?"

Frank leaned back against the edge of the porch floor, and crossed his arms across his hard-looking middle, his blue eyes sharp and searching, his thin gray hair fluffing around his forehead, his tanned skin looking leathery like

Jo's Uncle Toss's, almost like they were brothers. "I've known you since you was a little kid, and you oughtta know you can trust me like you did your daddy."

"I know, Frank. I do. But what I'm about to tell you is right there with all the other underhanded crap we've all fought against in the business for years."

"Lyin' and cheatin'? Actin' real mean and savage? Folks tryin' to set themselves up above everybody around 'em? Comes from pride, and greed, and wanting power and money. It just tears you apart a whole lot when there're horses takin' the brunt."

"That's exactly right."

"So?"

"I'm beginning to wonder if Dutton isn't using artificial insemination with semen from established stallions to make it look like three or four stallions who can't breed on their own are actually impregnating mares."

Frank Sperry looked at Michael without saying anything, while he peeled the shiny paper off a piece of spearmint gum. "What kinda infertility?"

"Irreversible. Trauma to the testicles. From getting kicked while breeding, or getting hung up on a fence. Occlusive tumors that keep sperm from traveling the tracks from both testicles. Influenza with long-lasting, high fevers. Even one case where it looks like testosterone was given too long and hasn't reversed over time. There're all conditions you can't diagnose visually. The horse'll look just fine. But they aren't going to be treatable. And Watcher, of course, who from what you and Dad say, is a strange case of his own."

"So the owners, they'd be doin' what? They'd be in it just for the stud fees?"

"That's one thing."

"'Course, you could get breedin' you can't normally afford by stealing semen from high-class stallions. Owners of high-stakes stallions pick and choose mares they're willing to breed to, and some mediocre bloodline mare could get bred above her class. Like you prob'ly figured."

"Yep."

"So the owners of those mares would have to be in on it too. That's alotta folks colludin', and alotta risk that news of it'll get out and about."

"I know."

"So it's not gonna be any stallion from Spendthrift Farm, or Claiborne, or Calumet, or the other real good barns. They got their own vets, and handle their bookings real close to their chest."

"Right."

"'Course Calumet, I ain't sure it's gonna be doing so well now, with Jimmy Jones retirin' and all, and Bull Lea dead. *He* was a stud to write home about."

"Just Citation alone. Not to mention all the rest."

"So you're thinkin' they'd have to be stealin' semen from decent stallions that mightta just been brought into some medium-level barns, where they don't have their own vets, and Dutton gets called in. Maybe owners who're new to the business, trying to step up real fast. Either that, or use just any old stallion so their own don't look like a dud."

"Yep."

"How do ya figure he'd pull it off?"

"He'd have to collect the semen, could be in a condom, saying he needs to do a whole collection during a live cover, 'cause he's worried about motility or something, and needs to do a lot of tests. Or he'd use what they always collect, when they're moving the stallion off, with the cup on the end of the stick."

"They'll always take that sample. Put it under a microscope right then and check there're no problems. Even though the semen you get is different at the beginning of the coverin', and during the middle, and at the end too. It still gives ya somethin' to go by. And it can help you see to plan another coverin' for that same mare a couple days later, if you think you're gonna need to. I reckon someday they'll have better ways to tell when a mare's in foal, but now it ain't so easy, and can take a lotta time."

"So what if he did that—gave his report to the farm folks, then poured the semen into a container when nobody else is watching, added some recipe of his own for an extender, and took it right over to the barn where he'd do the AI on another mare."

"Timing'd be important. Ya can't let the semen sit around."

"No. But on the days he's going to any one of the four barns where I think he's doing the AI, he does the 'breedings' in the late afternoon or early evening. He's always got a reason for that too. The stallion owner wants to be there. The mare can't be trailered over till late. Some reason to make it the end of the day. And there's always a big gap in his afternoon schedule when I can't find out where he's been. He could use his own stallion's semen, to substitute to get some mare in foal, but his stallion's nothing special, and nobody'd pay much for his stud fee. Except to make their own stallion look like he's fertile."

"Somebody might could do it, though. Somebody new to the business, with more pride than sense, might want to do that just so he didn't look like a fool for buying a stallion who ain't up to the job." Frank had rolled himself another cigarette, and he was slipping it in his shirt pocket to save for later in the day.

"It's not like with semen from a good breeding stallion the numbers are in your favor either. The chances of breeding a good racehorse are long no matter what."

"Sure, that's just part of the deal. So how do you figure you can prove what he's doin'?"

"There's no good way I can think of. I know one of the grooms at one of the barns, and I'm going to try to accidentally meet him at the bar he goes to Friday night and see what I can find out. Other than that, I'm going to try to case those suspect barns and see what the setups are. You know what it's like. The breeding barns are usually big empty spaces with a couple of big doors, and a lot of windows, and the padded partitions where they breed them plus a bench along one wall somewhere where they set up the microscope and do the final testing. So maybe I could follow Dutton to one of them and actually get a photo of him doing AI, or collecting semen, and taking it away."

"That don't sound easy."

"I don't think it will be."

"If I can help, you ask, ya hear? Don't know what I could do, but I'd be willing to try if you come up with a plan."

"Thanks. I appreciate it. He's done worse things than this too, and I'm trying to get his license jerked."

"Your ma know about this?"

"Yep."

"Then I trust Miss Margaret'll help come up with some kinda plan."

Wolf knew she was there before Michael did. He'd rushed into the living room before the pounding on the front door started, and he stood by the door, braced and growling, till Michael told him to sit and be quiet, as he turned on the porch light.

Michael saw her through the side panel by the wide black door—a sixtyish woman with straggling red hair, her eyes fixed and staring at him out of an angry face.

He told himself to be civil, and then opened the door, saying, "Marcella," without stepping back or motioning her in.

"You gotta talk sense to Ronnie. He won't listen to me, and he's gotta help pay for a lawyer!"

"It's one o'clock in the morning."

"So? I been here before when you weren't. I'm not waiting any longer. I need to come in and sit down."

Michael stood still, blocking the doorway, as he tied

his robe tighter around him. "How much have you had to drink?"

"Two Manhattans."

"That's all?"

"Yeah, that's all, though it's none of your damn business."

"Then you can drive yourself home. If it's more, I'll drive you myself."

"I told you that's all, and that's all. I'm not leaving here till I get some help."

"Yes. You are. I think Ronnie's absolutely right to not throw money away on your vendetta. And even if I didn't, he's a grown man, and it's none of my business."

"So you're just as—"

"Marcella, I'm going to bed. You go home and get some sleep. And believe me, I'm not changing my mind, so it's a waste of your time to come back here and try this again."

He shut the door and locked it while she shouted at him.

But five minutes later she walked away—then started her car and drove off.

Michael rubbed Wolf's chin and told him he'd been a very good boy, before he started toward the kitchen. "We might as well do something useful. I won't be getting back to sleep any time soon."

Michael sorted through the mail he'd left on the kitchen counter till he found the large manila envelope that'd

arrived that afternoon from a friend he'd made in the
army who now taught internal medicine at the University of Chicago's Med School.

There were three photocopies of articles on furosemide, the diuretic Dutton had ordered that had come in
from Germany. And Michael sat down on the window
seat at the small round table with the papers and a glass of
water.

An hour later he said, "*That's* interesting!" which
made Wolf pick up his head and stare sleepily at Michael
from his round overstuffed bed.

So furosemide, in humans, will not only work as a diuretic,
it'll reduce the risk of blood vessels breaking and bleeding in the
lungs.

You could use that for horses. If they could tolerate it. If it
performed the same way it seems to in humans. Exercise-in-
duced pulmonary hemorrhaging is not an insignificant condition.
If you could reduce the bleeding in the lungs that can happen
when they're racing, they'd be able to run faster. Theoretically.
Or at least as a possibility. And that would be something a vet
might try to get an edge on the track.

If you were the kind of vet who'd experiment with untested
drugs that haven't been accepted for equine use and aren't legal
on the track. And if I'm remotely right, Dutton's that kind of
vet.

Of course, I can't prove he got an illegal sample and injected
a horse. It's like everything else he does. You can speculate that
he's done it, but you can't come up with the evidence.

Michael yawned and stretched his arms out to the
side, knocking over his glass of water. He watched it

shatter on the hardwood floor, before he swore, and told Wolf to stay right there on his bed.

Wednesday, April 28th, 1965

Glenn Cook had swum for an hour at the "Y" in Lexington, then lifted weights at home, and put chicken legs in the oven before he showered and made a salad, and ate that with his mom's potato salad on the screened-in porch Jo had had built off to the right of his kitchen, just behind his living room.

He was now standing in his studio, wearing tan shorts and a cotton shirt he hadn't bothered to button, staring at the portrait of Cliff he'd sketched-in in pencil that morning, holding a glass of iced tea with mint he'd found growing by the porch when he'd moved in.

He carried the photo Meg had given him to the tall ratty leather chair that'd belonged to his mother's daddy, and let himself sink down slowly, while looking at the angle of Cliff's head and the shadows falling across him from the west. He studied the photos of the house he'd taken too, and looked back and forth at his sketch, before he gazed out the open French doors at the three red-winged blackbirds squabbling at the feeder in back.

Glenn had been thinking about the Cliff he'd known, and he could almost see him suturing cuts and giving shots to Baxter, the gelding Glenn had been riding when he'd been hurt—Cliff doing what he did well with a

quiet sort of humor that came right out of a straight face
to catch folks by surprise.

Then he remembered him, where he'd never expected to see him, in his own room at St. Joe's hospital, six
weeks after he'd been hurt.

It was one of the worst times after the accident, when
they still weren't sure they could save the leg, and they'd
had him on morphine for weeks on end, and all of it
taken together was making him angry and crazy. His
fiancée had handed him his ring back the day before,
then left to spend the summer in Tuscany, and he was
furious, in general, in a cast up to his waist, being waited
on like a baby, the skin rotting and itching like hell, and
his mother telling him he'd be just fine if he'd just learn
to be patient.

Cliff walked in, tall and broad and big boned, with
two books under his arm—*The Problem of Pain* and *Brat
Farrar*, without saying a word about why he'd picked
either—and stood quietly at the side of Glenn's bed
looking more serious than normal. He told Glenn first
that Baxter, who'd injured a hock when Glenn was hurt,
was responding well to treatment, that Glenn's next-door
neighbor was taking good care of him, and that Meg
would be up to see him later in the week.

Glenn hated to think about the way he'd reacted—
complaining and whining more than he had with anyone
else—while Cliff stood there and listened, his hands in
the pockets of his sport coat.

He'd stared at the ceiling, then read Glenn's chart
hanging on the foot of the bed, before he'd sat and

leaned toward Glenn, with his forearms resting on his knees. "The morphine's making everything worse. It distorts your emotions and limits the ability to think objectively."

"So I should get off of it, and put up with the pain while I wait for next week's operation?"

Cliff waited for a minute, and then sat up straight. "I don't know about your daddy, but I served in World War I. I saw a lotta folks shredded. Mutilated in appalling ways. Saw 'em in World War II later, same as you must've done, when the veterans came home."

Cliff stopped then and stared at the floor, and a strained, uncomfortable silence settled in between them. "Meg and I lost our daughter. Meg's folks lost three. My parents lost two boys. Your generation may be the first, because of the developments in medical science, that won't have to count on losing a child."

Cliff stood up and put his hands in his pants pockets as Glenn reached for his water. "There're choices, Glenn, we all have to make. And we've got more control over how things turn out than we sometimes think."

He'd left then, without either of them saying another word. And all Glenn could think to do in the next few weeks was read the books Cliff had left. And contemplate the choices in front of him, whether he liked them or not.

In the next two years—through all the operations and the months of rehab—he'd never thanked Cliff the way he wished he had. Though they did spend more time together than folks from different generations generally do, at least in their day and age, because Cliff kept treating Baxter, and helped Glenn arrange Baxter's sale to a long-time friend of Cliff's. And when Glenn had had his first one-man show in a gallery in Lexington, Cliff and Meg had bought a painting Glenn was glad he'd painted.

Now, as he thought about Cliff's painting—which he'd been doing when he woke in the night, and made his way through the day too—he wanted it to be the best work he'd ever done—for Meg, and Michael, and Cliff as well, for telling him what he'd needed to hear right at the time he'd needed it.

And right then, as he limped to the canvas to pick up his pencil and adjust the jawline, he heard a car slide to a stop in his gravel drive—and he draped a cloth across the easel.

He gave them both a glass of pinot noir, and poured himself one as well, then took them into the living room where it was cooler inside those thick brick walls than in the screened-in porch.

They talked about the running at Keeneland, that had ended not quite a week before, and the commissions Glenn had gotten from the paintings he'd hung in Keeneland's group exhibit. He'd sold more than he'd expected, and been given enough commissions, two of them from England, to keep him going through the fall.

Then Meg set her glass on the table by her chair and looked across at Michael. "You're the one who ought to tell him."

"I will in just a second." Michael was standing in front of the fireplace gazing at a painting of a reddish bay mare with black legs and mane and tail, with a kind eye, and a tiny foal who looked just like her, with a pastel land and cloudscape trailing off behind them. "I didn't know you owned a painting by Edward Troye." It was a horizontal canvas, a little over two feet wide, painted in 1833.

"It's from my mother's family. She's very distantly related to Troye on her mother's side, and she inherited that five or six years ago from an obscure cousin she'd never met. It's the only Troye I know of where we don't know the names of the horses. It's just called *Colonel William Ransom Johnson's Mare and Foal*."

"He knew a lot about horse physiognomy."

"Yeah, I think he did. He came from Switzerland, and painted horses all across Kentucky from the 1830s till he died in 1870-something. If we didn't have his work, we'd have almost no visual record of the famous early Thoroughbreds—Lexington, and all the others—that are still the foundation of the breed today. So what are you supposed to tell me?"

Michael did then—his theory about Dutton doing AI —and the need for some kind of proof, and the difficulty of getting it. "So Mom and I got to thinking that you may've been commissioned to do a painting of a farm, or a horse, or an owner from one of the implicated farms. We're interested in Golden Window Farm, Yellow Tree Farm, Ridgelee and Aldernay. Though it's almost too much to hope that you're doing work at any of them."

"So what do you want me to do?"

"Are you ready for this? We're actually hoping you could get yourself onto one of these farms and get a photograph of Dutton doing AI."

"Is that all?" Glenn laughed. Then looked from Michael to Meg. "You mean it, don't you?"

Neither of them said anything for a minute. Till Meg shook her head and said, "I know it's a lot to ask."

Glenn took another swallow of pinot noir, then set the glass on the end table next to him. "Nothing's been officially commissioned. But I have been approached by Harry Snyder, the guy who bought Aldernay last year. When we met four or five months ago, he didn't seem to me to know much about horses, or the business in general. He asked if I'd consider doing a painting of an old barn he's restored, with a groom and one of his stallions in front. I've told him I'd be happy to take a look at the location and the horse he selects, but I put him off till the fall. I s'ppose I could call him up and arrange to do it sooner. Tell him I don't have a day I could plan on right away, but I should in the next few weeks. Hoping that gives you time to find out when Dutton's going to go there for a breeding, so I can schedule at the same time. I have heard Mr. Snyder's been ill and has someone else overseeing the farm."

Meg said, "We haven't been able to see how Michael or I could insinuate ourselves onto one of the farms. Especially on a day when Dutton's there too, and actually get a picture of what's going on in the breeding barn."

"Not only that, we don't have photographic equipment that's up to the job, or the experience to pull it off." Michael was sitting on the sofa to the left of the fireplace, and he set his glass on the carved Chinese trunk Glenn used as a coffee table.

Meg nodded, turning sideways in her chair to look at Glenn in his. "It wouldn't be without risk. I don't know anything about this Harry Snyder, but Dutton's capable of terribly unprincipled behavior. He blackmailed one poor man who ended up taking his own life, and Dutton couldn't care less. Whether he'd be physically dangerous, I don't know. I've got no evidence that he would be, but I have to say it wouldn't surprise me."

"Well, I couldn't run away from him, but if he made the mistake of getting close, I swim enough laps and lift enough weights, I think I can fend for myself." Glenn laughed then.

And Meg and Michael did too, but there was something uncomfortable under Glenn's laughter, and Meg and Michael looked at each other without saying a word.

"So you'd need to tell me as far ahead as possible when Harris is scheduling a breeding at Aldernay." Glenn poured the last of the pinot into Michael's glass, and took another sip of his own.

"There isn't usually a whole lot of warning. The timing's based on the mare being ready. By that I mean that she's started ovulating, and you figure that out by palpating her, and you don't always have much warning."

"I'm flexible. It's not me. It's just giving Snyder a call, and saying I've got a last-minute opening when I could come and look at the barn. Especially if he's ill and not so involved in the running of the farm."

"I've been to Aldernay. With Dad, and on my own, for everyday vet work when Dutton couldn't go. I can draw you a map of how the barns are arranged. And if the timing's right, I could go with you, if I can find a way not to be seen by Dutton, but see what he's up to."

Meg said, "If you change your mind, we'll understand. This isn't your problem."

"Oh, yes it is. Trying to get rid of the crooks in the business is everybody's job."

Michael said, "Yeah, but—"

"I also owe Cliff a good turn. What you're doing is what he'd do if he were here."

"Why do you owe Cliff a good turn?" Meg had finished her wine and was staring at Glenn with a soft, startled look on her face he'd never seen before.

"He told me what I didn't want to hear when I needed to hear it."

"Yep. Dad was good at that. A man of few words who made them count. You know Ronnie Holmes, Glenn?"

"Not well, but I do, from after we found the confession in the wall."

"Well, Dutton's making his life a misery threatening to fire him if he says anything to Mom or me about anything wrong at the clinic."

"Sounds like an outstanding guy."

Meg smiled, and gazed at the fireplace as though she were off somewhere else. "Cliff did say what needed to be said, but he'd sometimes wait a long while. Once a year I'd do something that really irritated him, and he'd raise his voice when he told me about it. Every single time, I knew I had it coming. Perhaps not for whatever I'd done that moment, but for the hundreds of small selfish acts he'd quietly overlooked."

"He did that to me too. I hated it when I was young. Now I'm glad he did it." Michael laughed and smiled at Meg.

Who nodded and looked away.

CHAPTER EIGHT

Friday, April 30th, 1965

Mick Fisher was a groom Michael had known since he was a boy when he'd gone out on calls with his dad. He'd been a teenager when Michael had first met him, and Mick was in his forties now, and every Friday after he'd gotten paid he'd go into Lexington and have a few beers with folks he'd worked with at one barn or another, usually at Bud's Bar and Grill.

He'd been born knowing how to handle horses—to calm them down, and raise up the young ones. And he worked hard and was willing to do anything, but he had trouble working for anybody for long, and he'd either quit or get fired.

He'd gone to Louisville and New Orleans, up to Saratoga and Belmont, even some of the cheap tracks, Covington and some in Ohio, and barns too in Illinois. But he'd been back in Lexington for almost a year, and Michael had run into him at the last barn he'd been at.

He was at Yellow Tree Farm now, a nothing-to-write-home about operation, with three or four stallions and eight or ten mares, and he did work around the stables and grounds as well as tending horses.

The farm had been bought a couple of years before by a guy from New York City who put in an appearance every couple of months but didn't seem to be interested in taking the business seriously. It could've been a tax write-off, because plenty of folks use horse farms for that. But he did make a point of being there when they were running at Keeneland and at Churchill Downs. He never could've managed the operation himself, and he relied completely on a farm manager, who was nobody anybody in Lexington knew much about.

At least that's what Mick said when Michael ran into him in Bud's that Friday night. He'd been sitting at the bar listening to Gus, who was what most people would've called "slow" back then, who worked part-time at the local dump, and cleaned stalls anywhere he could find a job, and whose one claim to fame was that he could name the capital of every state—which he did nonstop every Friday night after he'd gotten paid, when he could hitch a ride to Bud's. Most people humored him and listened more than they wanted to. Though there'd be others other nights who'd mock him and scare him enough he'd run out and hitch a ride home.

Mick had bought Gus a hamburger to get something into him, and was trying to ease himself away when Michael walked over and asked if he could buy Mick a beer.

They moved to a table away from Gus and the jukebox, and they talked about Michael's dad for a while, how Mick had been sorry to hear he'd passed away, and would've been at the funeral if he'd been in town. Michael ordered a T-bone for both of them, talking him into letting him do it for old-time's sake, and the things he'd said about his dad.

Mick was tall and strong and his hands were huge and hard. His hair was a stiff sandy red, and his face was red too, the way fair-skinned folks can turn in the sun, plus maybe the beer and his blood pressure.

They talked about the past, and where Mick had been working down south and up north, and how he saw the farms changing, and the way folks were training now, and making breeding decisions. By the time they'd gotten through the steaks and baked potatoes, they were talking about Yellow Tree Farm, and the absentee owner, and the manager who was running it, and it sounded to Michael like Mick was getting restless and might be moving on again the way a lot of grooms do.

Mick talked about the two stallions he took care of, and the two mares as well—what he thought of them, and what their babies were like, and whether they'd ever amount to anything on the track.

Michael asked what Proper Introduction was like, the stallion Cliff had said had had a testicular trauma that made him infertile, though he didn't tell Mick his dad's diagnosis, waiting to hear what he'd say.

That's when Mick shook his head and ordered another beer. "You know, that's kinda a funny thing.

When we breed my two stallions to a mare from off the farm, we'll use the groom that comes with the mare, with me or maybe one other groom, and maybe once in a great while the mare's owner's vet. With mares from Yellow Tree it's just us two, me and another groom from the farm, 'cause these ain't high-stakes Thoroughbreds. They're just everyday, long-odds coverings with horses we can handle just fine.

"But when Proper Introduction's getting bred, your guy, what's his name? Harris? The older vet? He comes over with this assistant of his, and they take over the whole deal. It's always late afternoon too, or sometime into the evening, and I get told to do the feeding, and sweep up for the night, and get my ass on home. Seems real strange to me. And I don't think much of Harris's assistant, I can tell ya that right now. Likes to throw his weight around, and you know me, I take exception to some jackass showin' off."

Michael asked what the assistant's name was, and Mick didn't know, but the description was Dutton's guy, Webber Swede, from Louisville—short, squat, black-haired and loudmouthed with a funny way of talking out of more one side of his mouth than the other.

"Your dad, he liked this guy Harris? He figured he was a good vet?"

"Dad died six months after he hired him, and he didn't have a chance to know as much about him as he would have if he'd lived longer."

"There's somethin' about him. He ain't done nothin' to me. I got no reason to bitch. But if I need to call a vet,

you're the one I'll be askin' for, you can bet your boots
on that."

"Good. I'm glad to hear it."

"Even though you ain't hardly dry behind the ears."

They both laughed before Michael asked if Mick was
going to stay around Lexington, or move on again soon.

"I ain't seen my daughter in over a year. She's
workin' down in Ocala for a farm there. But I reckon I
might stay on through the fall, and move on after Keeneland's race week. 'Course that could change. But you
know what?"

"What?"

"If I see anything funny goin' on with Harris and the
jerk he brings with him, I'm gonna let you know. That's
what you want, right? You're lookin' worried to me,
boy, and I bet you come lookin' for me on purpose."

"That what you think?"

"Yep. That's what I think."

They both smiled before Michael finished his coffee.
Then he got up and paid the bill and watched Mick walk
back to the bar.

As Michael made his way through the crowd, and
then on out past the front door, a small man—thin and
sallow, sitting in the back of the bar—followed his every
move with deep-set pale-lashed eyes.

Saturday, May 1st, 1965

It was a little before four a.m. when Michael got the call

from Aldernay Farm. Dutton Harris was out of town.
Jerry was on call but at another barn, and one of Aldernay's older mares was having a difficult foaling that had
turned out to be a breech.

He smiled for a second, as he sat on the edge of the
bed and patted Wolf on the head. Getting a chance to
look at Aldernay without Dutton Harris around was
almost too good to be true.

It was a much more dangerous delivery than it should've
been, though Michael managed to save the colt and the
mare as well. Her waters had broken hours before, and
they should've called him then, or at least as soon as they
realized it would be a breech birth. Which meant he
didn't walk away with a great impression of the barn
manager, who for some reason seemed vaguely familiar,
though he couldn't remember ever meeting him.

But then, after he left the foaling barn, he drove out
to the west side of Paynes Mill Road—the east-west road
that intersected Pisgah Pike where Aldernay took up the
whole west corner of the crossroads—and pulled off next
to the fence on the edge of the road where it almost
backed up to the breeding barn.

He climbed the creosoted fence and stepped into the
cluster of trees that grew between there and the barn,
moving slowly from tree to tree, to the barn's south end,
where its big double door must've been not much more
than fifteen feet away from the edge of the woods. There
were double doors on the other three sides—he'd seen

that from the foaling barn—but if he had to bet, they'd be shut whenever Dutton "bred" Norseman. But this side they couldn't shut. The left half of the sliding door was hanging off its rollers—right where Glenn would have some cover in that pocket of trees.

Sunday, May 2nd, 1965

Laura and Michael went to the late service that morning, and then he dropped her at her folks, where they were having a big get-together that afternoon with some of her father's business associates.

Michael wanted to go back to the clinic and do some investigating while the office was closed. And when he got there he talked to the vet assistant who was monitoring three post-operatives—a gelding who'd had to have an eye removed, a mare who'd had a roar surgery, and another who'd had a bone chip removed from the outside of a fetlock. He looked at their charts and asked a few questions, and went on into reception.

He took the appointment book into his office and started looking for afternoon appointments Dutton had had at small and medium-sized farms that had at least one decent stallion.

He eliminated one after another—too early in the afternoon, or followed by other appointments at other places with clearly defined tasks—till he found one at Midway Farm, where he knew the farm manager reasonably well.

It'd been a fairly successful breeding operation on a modest scale, but the widower owner, Barclay Judd, had had a stroke six months before, and his only daughter lived in California, so the whole responsibility had fallen on Dave Rattigan.

Michael thought about calling him, but decided to just drive over and see if he could talk to Dave in person.

He unlocked both gates, and locked them behind him, then drove on to the manager's house, which was a tenant house in the back of the property that'd been added on to and fixed up really well not too many years before.

Dave's wife opened the door, with her five-year-old son squinting at him from behind her skirt, and told Michael that Dave was walking the long lane between the paddocks trying to find a sharp piece of fence. "One of the mares sliced her lip on something and he's looking for where it could've happened."

"Do you think he'd mind if I go look for him?"

"No. He'll be glad to see you."

Dave was half a mile away leaning over a fence corner where one of the creosoted boards had had a thick splinter standing out from the surface right where a horse would poke itself one way or another. He'd pulled it off with pliers and was smoothing the edge with a wood file.

"Hey, Michael. It's been too long." He was medium sized and muscular, with gray in his hair at forty, wearing aviator shades and a baseball cap, with a khaki shirt and jeans. "Want to walk the fence with me?"

"Sure."

"It's been awhile since I've done it myself, and it's good to get out and see how well the work's getting done."

"It is."

Michael asked how Barclay Judd was recovering from the stroke. And Dave said he was almost entirely house-bound now, and had to have somebody with him all the time, a real nurse part of each day, and a help-companion the rest.

"The daughter wants him to move to California, but he doesn't want to go. It's sad watching him try to talk. He understands what you're saying to him, but he can't say anything but yes and no. He had such a way with words before. He read all the time and was a born story-teller, so it must be making him crazy. He's in a wheel-chair he can push himself, but he can't get in and out of it on his own."

"What do you think will happen?"

"The daughter's married, and her life's out there, and I reckon they'll end up selling the farm, and he'll move there whether he wants to or not. He's not willing to do it now. And he likes to come out and get wheeled around so he can look at the horses and watch the birds, but you can't expect him to make the decisions the way he used to do."

"No, you wouldn't think he could. Not unless he can write instructions, and follow the finances and discus-sions."

"He can't write a word on his own. And I think the financials are pretty much beyond him. I read him reports and send contracts to his lawyers, but I'm not comfortable making all the decisions. He'd never fault me, but I'm not so sure about the daughter."

"It can't be an easy situation."

"No."

They walked for a while without much conversation, the two of them watching the mares and the babies, pointing out confirmation in the yearlings, discussing the daddies and what Dave hoped from combining the bloodlines, and then he stopped and took out his pipe and tamped tobacco in the bowl. "How are things with you?"

"They've been better, to tell you the truth."

"Your mom's okay, though?"

"Yeah. She's fine. But I wanted to ask you about a visit Dutton Harris paid here. There was a three o'clock afternoon appointment back on April 1st. What was he coming here for? And was there anything unexpected that happened during the appointment?"

Dave Rattigan lit his pipe and studied Michael through the haze. "He was coming to palpate two mares and see if they were ready to breed. I asked for you, but he came, and I didn't feel like I could tell him to leave. We needed it done that day."

"Sure. That's the way it is."

Dave didn't say anything. And Michael asked again if anything had happened he hadn't expected.

"Yeah, there was something. He asked to see Saracen.

He's getting older as you know, and he's not breeding as much as he once did, and he needs more attention in general, but he's bred some fine foals in his day, a few of them who raced really well."

"Archer's Friend and Westlake."

"Yeah, those two in particular. So anyway, Harris asked to see Saracen. He said he'd been a bit worried by the motility in the sperm sample you took the last time you bred him, when he saw the results in the file. He thought that since he was here already, he ought to do a complete collection with a condom and then perform some further tests."

"What did you say?"

"I didn't know what to do. I had to decide on my own, and I let him go ahead. We had an experienced mare who was ready to be bred and I let him do the collection. Funny thing was, he didn't just set up his microscope here like y'all generally do, he took the whole collection away with him, and took a blood sample from Saracen too."

"Really."

"Yeah. I asked him why, and he said he wanted to make sure Saracen wasn't fighting some disease and was still up to the job."

"Interesting. What time did he get done?"

"He got here a little before three and prob'ly left a quarter after four. Maybe even closer to five, I can't say for sure." Dave was relighting his pipe. He didn't actually smoke it all that much. He spent most of his time doing something to it, tamping the tobacco, scraping out the bowl, fiddling with the matches. "So why did you want to know?"

"I want to make sure that the people who represent us are treating the clients the way my dad would want."

"He's not like your dad, or you either one, I can tell you that for sure."

"Would you be willing to write out what you told me?"

Dave Rattigan stared at Michael, and then started walking toward his house, slapping away a horsefly that'd settled on his arm. "I'll have Ginny type it. I'll have her sign it too, that this was in my own words. There's a groom at the barns too who watched and listened to the whole thing with Harris. We could get him to sign too."

"If it's not too much trouble, that'd be great."

"You're not going to tell me what's got you worried. But I figure it's something important or you wouldn't've come here and asked."

"Well—"

"I've got no complaints about the service from Dutton. He's done his job okay when he's been here, but there was something funny about taking that collection, and it's worried me some ever since. I don't want to be held accountable for anything he could be doing that isn't on the up-and-up."

"Did he give you the results of the tests he took?"

"A week later an assistant called and said the tests were normal."

"You know who?"

"No. The name went in one ear and out the other. It

was a woman, I remember that. Sounded young and kinda hesitant."

When he was driving over to Laura's, after having picked Wolf up, Michael asked himself why Dutton would've taken a blood sample.

The answer came two seconds later.

If he was using the sperm to inseminate a mare that hadn't been bred to Saracen before, he'd want to know if their blood was compatible. If she hadn't had a foal they'd be okay. But if she had, they could be incompatible and the foal would be in danger, kinda like the Rh factor in people when one parent's Rh negative and the other parent's positive. If he mixed their blood together and it clotted, he'd know he couldn't breed them together. I should've thought of that before.

Monday, May 3rd and Tuesday, May 4th, 1965

It was Monday when Michael found out that Dutton was scheduled to go to Aldernay at seven Tuesday night, and he called Glenn as soon as he knew. Glenn phoned the owner right away, and was actually able to talk to him and arranged to meet him Tuesday afternoon and tour the buildings on the farm.

It was a little after five when Glenn drove south to Aldernay on Pisgah Pike, where the entrance to the drive to the house led in from the east, though there was a separate drive to the stallion and broodmare barns from Paynes Mill on the south.

Mr. Snyder had told him to drive straight to the house, and Glenn's first thought when he saw it was he hoped Jo hadn't seen it. Mr. Snyder wasn't responsible. He'd bought it fully formed—a self-conscious inept attempt at old pillared proportions with tackily overdone everything that fought the original Federal restraint, as though someone in the thirties had had more money than taste.

But the inside was cool on a very hot day, and the foyer was open and uncluttered, and the housekeeper was pleasant when she took him into the study to wait for Harry Snyder—who came in five minutes later looking thinner and frailer and considerably older than he had when they'd first met.

They discussed the restoration he'd done of the broodmare barn, and the other buildings on the property, but mostly they talked about Highlander, the stallion Mr. Snyder wanted Glenn to paint.

He did agree, after they'd discussed the size of the portrait and the cost involved too, to let Glenn visit all the barns and buildings and offer his suggestions for where the painting should be set. And then, when Glenn asked, he wrote him a letter he could show the manager and the grooms if he were questioned that gave him permission to look at what he'd like, and arrange for a groom to take him to meet Highlander as well.

Mr. Snyder told him he wasn't able to be in Lexington as much as he'd intended; that business and personal matters were keeping him up in Boston, and he was having to rely on Mort Swede, his farm manager, more than he'd expected. He said he used to enjoy taking part in the breeding from time to time, but he hadn't been able to recently, though he hoped to again.

He wished Glenn well, asked him to report back and say where he'd like to set the portrait, and give him an estimate of when he could get started. He looked as though walking wasn't easy for him, as he led Glenn to the front door, telling him one of his stallions would be breeding a mare at seven, so seeing the breeding barn should be done before that.

Glenn asked what stallion it was, and was told what he already knew, that it was Norseman, who, according to Cliff, was permanently infertile because of a benign tumor that blocked both tracks.

Mr. Snyder kept a hand on the doorframe as Glenn limped through, then smiled and shook his hand. "Norseman wasn't a Grade 1 winner by any means, but he was here when I bought the farm, and I've become quite attached to him. He's a gentleman. And he's sensible. And if he doesn't actually earn his keep, he's at least producing a couple of foals and keeping his line alive."

Glenn said, "I've had horses myself I kept because of their personalities, even when they weren't fun to ride. Thank you again. I'll call you tomorrow, after I've had a chance to develop my film, so we can discuss what I've seen."

"I'll only be here through Saturday, so let's be sure to speak before that."

Glenn did have to show his letter to the manager and one of the grooms so he could look at all the barns. He fed Highlander a carrot from the feed room, before he photographed him out in the light, being held and positioned by his groom.

He took several shots of each side of the broodmare and foaling barn, which was Snyder's preference for the portrait, and various views of all the other barns, including the breeding barn.

It was six thirty when he finally left, before Dutton Harris had arrived, and he drove away on the south side of the farm along the west side of Paynes Mill. He parked half a mile away, pulled off into an overgrown drive that led into a patch of scrubland that looked like it'd once been a tobacco farm, where he could hide his car in a copse of self-seeded trees.

He waited there, till he saw a MacInnes pickup drive by, then waited another few minutes before he limped, slowly and carefully, along the side of the road, his Nikon hanging from his neck.

It was harder for him to climb the southwest fence than it had been for Michael, but he took his time, and chose a well-concealed place, and made his way into the trees.

They were thick there on the south side, pines and maples and redbuds too, growing into each other's sides, the ground around them needing trimming, as though the grounds crew had let it go.

He waited and watched through the broken west side of that south door, using his longest telephoto, and finally, once they'd brought in the mare, he could see her clearly, positioned between the padded mounting partitions, her flanks facing east. A stallion was being held by a groom beyond her by the far door, thirty feet, or maybe even more, well away from the mare.

And then Dutton Harris was there, looking at a slide under a microscope on a counter off on the right. Though what he did next Glenn couldn't see, for he'd moved closer to the southeast corner.

And then he was there again, shoving her tail to the assistant standing by her right flank. Glenn could clearly see the large syringe in Harris's gloved hand with a foot-long narrow rod where a needle would normally have been—and even before he inserted it in her vagina, Glenn was snapping photos that showed it, reasonably well-lighted from electric lights, as well as windows and skylights and the open door.

Dutton injected the contents of the syringe, while the mare held steady, looking totally unconcerned. And then as Dutton moved away, pulling off his surgical gloves, Glenn began to back through the trees as silently as he could.

But before he'd almost gotten to the fence, where he couldn't see the barn at all, the assistant who'd been holding the mare's tail was standing outside the broken south door, staring hard through the tangled trees, as though he wasn't sure what he'd seen, before he said something to Dutton over his left shoulder.

Wednesday, May 5th, 1965

It was almost six when Glenn drove out to Meg's and found she wasn't home. He'd been phoning her, and Michael too, since a little after five, but hadn't gotten an answer. He'd thought she might be doing something outside, and it might be worth the drive.

But then Jo might know where they were, and he drove back to her house, where he found Jo's Uncle Toss, and Jo and Alan too, sitting in the backyard underneath a shade tree in front of their small farm pond, with Ross shoving a tiny green truck in circles through the grass.

Jo stood up and waved, and asked if he'd like an iced tea.

Alan said, "We've got strawberries from Toss's garden too if you'd like a bowl with cream." Alan was six four and broad shouldered, and he was stretched out in an Adirondack chair with a bowl and spoon in his lap.

"Thanks. But not tonight. I'm trying to find Meg and Michael."

Toss said, "They're doin' some target shootin' over by Flintville. There's a place that belongs to a fella they know that's set up like a range." Toss was patting Emmy, the boxer-mutt, who'd said hello to Glenn when he'd arrived, then laid back down in the shade.

"You know when they'll be back?"

"Not really. But I could draw you a map. Or Jo could, either one." Toss was shading his eyes with his hand, his skin the color of saddle leather, as he squinted up at Glenn.

"I would like a map. Thanks."

Jo leaned over and checked Ross's diaper, then said she'd go in and make him one.

Glenn said, "So how are you, Toss? I haven't seen you in months."

Alan said, "He's as ornery as usual," and pointed at a great blue heron that had just flown over the pond.

Toss looked at Alan and laughed. "Yeah, I prob'ly am. 'Course, I been workin' my fingers to the bone with the new foals, and tryin' to get the yearlings ready for the owners to take to the summer sales, and with Jo redoin' houses all the time, and taking care of the squirt over there, I'm hard put on my own."

Alan said, "You have help. And you'd complain if she didn't do houses, and take care of Ross."

"I would. I like to see a woman workin'."

Alan said, "You better watch yourself," and laughed.

"Tell ya the truth, I like seein' her do what she loves." Glenn asked Toss how long it would take him to get to where they were shooting.

"Twenty minutes maybe. 'Course I could give you a shortcut that—"

"Toss's shortcuts have been known to get folks lost." Jo laughed and touched Toss on the shoulder, before she handed Glenn her hand-drawn map and settled her sunglasses on her nose. "Any chance you could come for dinner Saturday night?"

"Sure. Thanks."

Toss said, "When you get to where they're shootin? It's a pretty steep hill with a real good range partway up, and you can climb on up without worrying about gettin' shot."

"Thanks. That makes me feel a lot better."

It wasn't an easy climb for Glenn, but he paid attention to the footing, and hollered that he was on his way up, after a long burst of firing had stopped.

Meg and Michael were standing on a horizontal ledge where part of the hill had been bulldozed at one end, so they were shooting with the hill on their left and a deep dirt backstop straight in front of them. They'd stuck paper targets on bales of straw there, and arranged their gun boxes and ammunition on a collection of logs that were standing up on end on their left against the hill.

It took Glenn by surprise for a minute, seeing Meg with her calf-length skirt and sensible shoes and her white hair pulled back in a bun fitting bullets into the cylinder of a .38 Smith and Wesson.

"I know. What's a retired lady from Georgia doing shooting a gun at my age?"

"Well—"

"My aunt was a farm lady who'd shot varmints all her life, and she taught me when I was young. It's something Michael and I can do for fun."

Glenn said, "I give you credit for keeping up with it. I still shoot skeet once in a while myself. But what I came for was to give you both copies of the photographs I developed last night. Either of you have a safe? I don't, and I thought—"

"I brought my office safe home when I retired." Meg set the safety on her .38, then laid it down on a stump.

"Good. Then I'll give you the negatives too. I don't like the thought of these being in my darkroom with nothing but a lock on my front door. I had to play with the contrast and do some fairly complicated enlargement work to get them as clear as they are."

They were very clear, and all three of them stood and stared at twelve eight-by-ten photographs, eight of which showed Dutton Harris at different stages of injecting something from a large syringe with a tube on the end into a mare's vagina, while his assistant held her tail and a groom held her halter.

There were photos of another horse, who looked like a stallion because of his arched neck, being held beyond her on the other side of the barn, and a carrying case too sitting on the bench by the microscope, where another print showed Dutton slipping a slide under the micro-scope before he did the injection. Each print was numbered chronologically on the back with a time and date as well, and Glenn also gave them two pages of notes that described his visit to Aldernay, and what Mr. Snyder had told him about Norseman getting bred.

Michael said, "I can't believe it. You caught him right at it!"

"I don't know how much they prove, though. He's not breeding Norseman, true. He's injecting a substance into a mare. He checked a slide of something before he went ahead, which could've been semen he'd brought from another stallion to check for motility before he did the insemination. But how can you actually prove there's sperm in that syringe?"

Michael shrugged, then brushed away a fly. "I don't know. But we're closer than we were. Thank you. I can't believe it went as well as it did."

Meg stared at one print after another before she slipped them back in the envelope. "We can't thank you enough."

"It was actually easier than I thought, because of where the breeding barn is. Michael prepared me really well with the location of the trees, and the barn, and the broken door. Now, the guy holding the stallion that I think is Norseman, is the barn manager. The groom holding the mare's tail came with Harris. The one holding her halter came with her from Windemere, which I don't know anything about. From what I gathered when I was eavesdropping in the broodmare barn, it may be a new barn up near Louisville."

Michael said, "The city where Dutton worked for years. One thing I do know is where he went this afternoon. I followed him when he left the clinic. I happened to see him leave, and I didn't have anything I had to do right then that I couldn't postpone. Anyway, he went over to Ladyfield and bred a very good stallion there. I was able to park so I could use my binoculars and see the stallion being led across to the breeding barn and his name was in huge letters on his fly sheet. Ulysses's Son. He's the one Dutton usually breeds there, so if I had to bet, this was a case of him stealing the sample from the cup-and-stick that he'd test after the breeding. I can't believe that barn would be willingly doing AI."

Glenn said, "No. But the mare's owner, the mare who was bred at Aldernay, he's got to be in on it, don't you think? He's paying for better sperm for a not impressive mare that he couldn't get any other way. Or at least maybe as cheaply."

"That's what I think too. The guy holding the mare's tail, by the way, that's Dutton's boy Webber Swede."

Meg said, "Seems to me being honest would be a great deal easier, and a whole lot less nerve-wracking."

Glenn smiled and set his hands on his hips. "Some folks love the thrill of doing what they shouldn't."

Meg said, "That's true. Why would I forget, when I've seen it all my life? Could I talk you into coming home for dessert? Toss gave me some strawberries, and I've made homemade shortcake."

When Glenn got home a little after ten, he pulled up in front of his porch and took longer getting out of the car than usual. He was stiff and sore, much worse than normal, from the walking he'd done at Aldernay and climbing up and down the hill that evening as well.

He reset the hinge on his leg brace and stepped up on the big uncut stones Jo had stacked as steps—first one, and then the other—grabbing on to a porch post before he limped to the door.

And then, when he got ready to unlock his door, he saw it'd been left unlocked.

He would've sworn he'd locked it before he left. And when he stepped inside and stood for a minute in the silvery dark, he listened and watched what he could, before he turned on the lights. The house sounded the way it should, silent and empty.

And when he stepped into the library-dining room, through the archway on his left, it looked the way he'd left it, once he'd switched on the lights.

He walked past the front stairs into the living room across from the library, and turned on the lamp by the door. Everything was where he'd expect it and didn't look disturbed.

He went on into his studio, through the door to the right of the living room fireplace, afraid now of what he'd find, where everything he valued most had been left open and exposed.

He flipped on the light switch and grabbed the back of his grandfather's chair, while he stood and scanned the room. Cliff's portrait was untouched on the easel. The paints and brushes were right where they ought to be. The photos Meg had given him of Cliff, and the ones he'd taken with her at the house, were still spread out on the table to the left of the easel.

Then he looked past the studio fireplace, off beyond it on his left, and saw the door to his darkroom closed the way he'd left it.

He limped across, holding on to the mantel, and pulled the door all the way open—and found his files of

negatives and prints, his enlarging and cropping equipment, his chemicals and his mixing containers right
where they should've been on counters and in cabinets—
once he'd opened their doors.

He'd left three envelopes of prints on the counter
though, above the files on the left side of the room—
photographs of his sister's family he'd be giving her that
weekend; shots of his mother's gardens she'd asked him
to take; photographs he'd taken at Keeneland during the
racing that spring.

His mom's and his sister's envelopes were still there
exactly where he left them, but the shots he'd taken of
the runners at Keeneland weren't anywhere on the
counter.

He moved stacks and searched through drawers, and
then stood back with his hands on his hips and stared at
that whole wall.

And then he saw the corner of a small manila envelope sticking out from the left edge of the file cabinet
right where it met the floor—and he leaned down and
pulled it out from where it'd slipped behind the back.

The photos from Keeneland.

Right where they shouldn't have been.

*Could I have knocked them off when I was gathering up
everything else to take to Meg and Michael?*

*No. I know I straightened the counter afterwards, and laid
those three in a row.*

"Michael? Sorry to call so late. Someone went through

my darkroom while I was gone tonight… No, it wouldn't be that hard. I don't have a garage. I have to park in front, so if someone watched from up by the road, even if they had to use binoculars, they'd know when I was gone… The door was unlocked when I got home too, and I'd swear I locked it when I left. It wouldn't be that hard to open it if you knew what you were doing, with picks, or whatever they call them, without doing any damage… Yep. It's something we better think about, and talk again tomorrow."

Glenn had hung up, and was standing in his kitchen drinking a glass of water, when he found himself seeing Dutton's assistant—his dark hair and thick black eyebrows, his skewed, twisted, lopsided face—staring across the mare's hindquarters while he'd snapped his last few shots.

CHAPTER NINE

Excerpt from Jo Grant Munro's Journal
Friday, May 7th, 1965

Michael and Meg, and Glenn too, think Dutton Harris must've been behind the break-in at Glenn's house. Not that he'd go himself. He'd probably send his assistant from Louisville, whose name escapes me at the moment. Glenn's bet is that guy, who was pretty much facing him while he took the pictures, must've seen him right as he was leaving Aldernay. He was sure he hadn't seen him earlier on, but maybe when he moved back through the trees. And they all assume he was looking for the photographs Glenn took of the so-called breeding.

There was almost no evidence anyone had been there, so Glenn didn't call the police. Anybody today would've worn gloves. And I think he's just thanking God none of his art was damaged.

Dutton Harris walked into the clinic file room when he knew no one else was there and searched through the "M" drawer till he found the "Metzger, Wesley" file, and took it into reception.

He told Eliza, who was answering the phone that morning, of two changes in his schedule for the afternoon, before she told him his mother had called when he was with a patient.

"If she calls again tell her I'll call her sometime this weekend, and that she's not to phone me here at work unless it's an emergency. This is not the first time I've told her that, as I think you well know."

Dutton stepped into his office and closed the door behind him, then sat down at his desk. He sorted through the Metzger file till he found the medical reports from two farm visits he'd made, one in February and one in April. He read through them quickly and slipped them in his briefcase, then pulled two blank exam forms out of his righthand drawer. He filled them out in four or five minutes and tucked them into the file, then took it into the file room and dropped it back where it belonged.

It was a little after midnight when Dutton got home from Louisville. He parked his Jaguar XKE in the garage next to the clinic pickup, then stepped into the hallway between the kitchen and the dining room. He locked the three locks on the door to the garage and walked down the hall to the living room.

He dropped his keys on the console table that stood

to one side of the front door and told himself not to look at it—the hideous hollow-core molded door that opened right into the living room in this pedestrian brick fifties ranch he'd never imagined himself owning.

He'd tried to create some sense of a foyer by setting the round Queen Anne table he'd inherited from his mother's family in the middle of the front half of the living room, having arranged the only seating area with his leather sofa and two chairs by the fireplace in back.

He'd set *The Patriot* on the round table too—the foot-high bronze by Augustus Saint-Gaudens he'd inherited from his father's drunken father, who, like his father before him, had squandered the rest of his inheritance.

Dutton let his fingers slide down the deep folds of *The Patriot's* cloak, then pulled off the tie he'd slung around his neck when he'd thrown on his clothes at Annette's.

He slipped the Accutron off his wrist while he walked into the bedroom, then took off his belt and unbuttoned his shirt, on his way to wash the smell of her off first, before he got rid of the reports.

He pulled on a pair of silk boxer shorts and slipped his arms into a matching pajama top, then carried his briefcase into the living room and laid it on the tan leather sofa, where he pulled out the medical reports he'd taken away that morning.

There were wooden matches in a silver julep cup on

the plain pine mantelpiece, and he struck a match on the bricks beside it and lit one corner of all four sheets and watched them burn to ash in the grate.

He took his briefcase into his office and laid it on top of his sleek black desk, then opened the door of the bedroom closet he'd turned into shelving and storage. He dialed the combination of the black metal safe that took up the whole left side—its bottom third fitted with an office file, the rest with gray metal drawers.

He opened the lowest and looked into several of the two dozen watch boxes, touching the elegant faces and thinking about how he'd tracked them down and negotiated the prices, before he picked up his Vacheron Constantin from 1952. He slid his finger along the rounded corners of the square gold case and the pattern in the alligator band. Then he wound it carefully and stared at it for half a minute and laid it back in its box.

He took out his favorite Patek Phillipe, a gold 1932 Calatrava with another sleek black band. It was slim and minimalist, in honor of the Bauhaus movement, and he wound it and set it back, before he picked up a 1953 Rolex—the Submariner, with a black face and radium-filled dots and sticks. He set the time and wound it, then fastened the stainless-steel oyster band on his right wrist, before he sorted through the tray of antique pocket watches, picking up one after another, admiring the elegance and the precision of the watchmakers, and the artists who'd painted his one enamel portrait face, as well as a landscape on another.

He stood there for another ten minutes staring at the

clear plastic boxes filled with gold coins in sealed transparent strips divided into individual pockets that were lined up in straight rows in two of the deeper drawers. Gold was only thirty-six dollars an ounce, but the day was coming when it would be worth much more, and it did have certain advantages. He could trade it anywhere in the world, under the table as well as above, and none of the coins he owned now could be traced as payment for services rendered.

He pulled out a box of British sovereigns, organized by date from 1957 to 1965, and counted the strips, smiling to himself, before he opened the last drawer where bound stacks of small bills were arranged by value, front to back. He touched each stack before he closed the drawer, then locked the safe and twirled the dial, enjoying the feel in his fingers, and the clicking of the turning mechanism as it revolved in his hand.

He padded barefoot down the hall to the dining room and poured two fingers of Maker's Mark into a crystal cocktail glass, then walked through the hall and the rear half of the living room to the screened-in porch in back.

He settled himself in his new teak settee, rearranging the down cushions, as he swallowed a quarter of his bourbon, savoring the caramel and the lingering vanilla and the fire that warmed the whole center of his insides, with a long slow sigh.

He gazed at the glowing hands on his Rolex and listened to the sounds in the fields—the wind sifting through softly shifting trees, his stallion and his two mares wandering their separate paddocks, while a thin strip of shimmering cloud swept in front of the moon.

And then he was lost in it, the way he had been driving from Louisville. The interference and the growing hostility. The plotting and the pretension. Talking to himself the way he always did, when there was no one else he could trust.

This Glenn Cook the photographer. His having become involved has escalated the opposition to a level that's much more threatening. Michael must be running an investigation that's way more aggressive than I thought. And that, of course, is no small matter when my future depends on the clinic.

It's never made sense to start my own practice. The outlay's more than I'd consider, with equipment costs the way they are now and the competition that's established.

That was the appeal of joining MacInnes. I could concentrate on Thoroughbred clients, where growth potential exists. I could buy shares gradually, while managing operations in such a way that the clinic would pay increasing returns—since I'd already proven to my own satisfaction that a great deal of money can be made if one is not restricted by the Thoroughbred establishment's unrealistic standards.

It's ridiculous that artificial insemination isn't endorsed for Thoroughbreds. The Quarter Horse and Saddlebred authorities see the advantages of controlling sexually transmitted disease, and the chances of injury that come with live covers, yet the Jockey Club and the racing establishment resist all change. They're petrified at the thought of losing stud fees, and related breeding revenue, if they alter their age-old traditions. And that gives me an opportunity to maneuver outside their archaic restrictions to great personal advantage.

Even so, the MacInneses' posturing has become nearly unbearable. Clifford's expertise and personal integrity cannot be matched by any other mortal. While Meg's and Michael's hushed tones when putting forth the standards that must be adhered to, based, of course, on what has gone before, make me feel nearly savage enough to say and do what would drive them both to sever my employment right away. And now, insisting that their favorite clients be allowed to continue paying their bills over time, that's a form of interference I can't tolerate for long.

Why can't either of them see that the profitability of the practice could be increased substantially by fairly simple everyday procedures that are practiced by many in the field? Worshipping the past is limiting our profitability and keeping us from moving forward into a changing future.

Once I'm able to acquire shares in September, the destiny of the clinic could become mine to control. Meg is in her seventies. If her death were to occur, it wouldn't be unexpected. And Michael, of course, has no heirs to inherit the stock he owns—if he were to be swept from the field before he marries and has children. As the only other shareholder, my way forward would be essentially assured—depending, of course, on what they've learned and how they plan to respond.

And that, of course, is the critical question. What does Meg intend to do? She could fire me at any time, and yet she's made no move. That leads me to assume she's waiting to gather evidence of actual wrongdoing. She may intend to compromise my position within the profession. And if that's true, I shall have to take matters into my own hands before the situation worsens. Therefore, the obvious importance of the Metzger files.

They can't prove I performed artificial insemination on the mare at Aldernay. I shall say that I was treating her for a uterine infection—simply using the infusion rod attached to the syringe to instill an antibiotic into the uterus, as any veterinarian would. I shall have to tell the manager there the explanation I'm giving. Though Webber can do that easily without me getting involved. He's his stepbrother, after all, and he'll go along without a quibble. I would have to come up with an explanation for the presence of the stallion. Though that shouldn't be too hard once I put my mind to it.

Of course, if Michael's seen me do a complete collection here with a condom on my own stallion, and then take it away to one of the other barns, that would be hard to explain. And it wouldn't be impossible for him to observe me. The placement of the barn. The windows facing the drive. I've never seen any indication that he's followed me home, but if he's grasped the fact that I'm doing AI, he must've considered the possibility that I'd use my own horse's semen to keep some client's infertile stallion from being publicly exposed.

Which leads me inevitably to how systematic is Michael's investigation? It was one thing when the Yellow Tree groom called to tell me he'd seen Michael talking to Mick Fisher in a bar in Lexington. But arranging for the photographer to follow me—that's a much more alarming indication of what Michael and Meg are doing.

And what if he's learned that I brought the semen to Aldernay from Ladyfield? The photographer could've caught me checking a slide in the microscope before I approached the mare.

Though that in itself wouldn't be incriminating. Explanations could certainly be given. And Michael could've seen nothing on the schedule to indicate I'd been at Ladyfield. He would've had to follow me. But he wouldn't hesitate if he could do it without being seen.

He knows I put the stallion down on the plane to Florida, though he has no way of proving it was done for the insurance. Though the groom poses a threat. If he talks despite being warned.

I suppose Michael could have contacts in Louisville who could bring up the death of that mare three years ago. There was a vet assistant who did suspect I'd administered an overdose of insulin. Though the half-owner who arranged it, who didn't want to pay for her scheduled surgery, he wouldn't say a word. The other partner who became suspicious, he certainly might.

And what about Rain Tree Farm and contacts they could have there?

If Michael's able to get concrete data, they could try to get my license revoked, and that's a risk I can't take. I will not make my father's mistakes. Now, or in the future.

I will not spend the rest of my life with an arm up the rectum of a horse. I will move home to Virginia and live a life I choose. I will travel where and when I wish, and pursue my own particular interests the way my parents' families did before the Depression robbed them of the lives they'd been raised to expect.

Of course, the more immediate issue is if you want to see Annette again, you should phone her tomorrow afternoon.

Tuesday, May 11th, 1965

Ronnie Holmes was heading toward his car asking himself how much longer he could take the condescending looks and the snide remarks. There hadn't been an out-and-out fight. He hadn't done anything that gave Harris a reason to let him go. It was just an everyday series of pinpricks to make sure he knew the scrutiny he was under.

He used to wake up raring to get to work, but now he could hardly stand it. And everyone was feeling the same, you could see it in their eyes. And what was even worse was that normal medical procedures were falling by the wayside.

Just the petri dishes—they were a good example. Three of them. Shoved in the back of the spare oven with no identification. The horse's name should've been on the lid, with the date the sample was taken. And he could tell they weren't on ordinary agar, and that should've been on the lids too. Not following proper procedure meant mistakes were easy to make, especially with several folks setting up the tests.

Michael and Jerry hadn't cultured them, and Deb knew nothing about them, so that left the other two assistants he hadn't had a chance to ask.

And then Ronnie heard his name called in a high reedy voice just as he got to his truck, and he turned and saw Samuel Freemantle sidling unsteadily toward him.

Ronnie said, "Crap!" under his breath, and set his lunchbox on the seat of his truck, before he started toward the cousin who'd inherited everything Glenn had found in his bedroom wall. "Sam! I haven't seen you since—"

"You donated a copy of the unsubstantiated confession to the Woodford County Historical Society!" Samuel Freemantle was short and stout and probably sixty, and his suit looked as though it'd been asked to hold more than it comfortably could. His thin gray hair was plastered on his egg-shaped head, and his small eyes looked restless, shifting from place to place.

Ronnie chose not to answer back. He just walked on toward Sam and tried to smile.

"There's a matter I need to discuss with you. A personal matter I would never raise if circumstances didn't demand it." Sam had been moving slowly, and he was sweating more than Ronnie would've expected, and he dabbed a handkerchief across his face before he stopped by his side. "I'm about to undergo a surgical procedure at a medical facility in Minnesota that involves a considerable degree of risk. I tell you this not to engage your sympathy, but because it behooves me to make certain plans before that event takes place."

"I'm sorry, Sam. Have you told my mom?"

"It will not have escaped your notice that your Aunt Marcella and I have had more than one confrontation concerning the unsubstantiated confession and the distribution of the heirlooms that were found in the wall in my former home."

"Yeah, I guess you'd say I've noticed." Ronnie grinned before he could stop himself.

And Sam looked displeased. "You're also aware that I have no descendants."

Ronnie nodded, wondering why Sam was talking to him like he never had before.

Sam was silent then, for more than a minute, as he wiped the sweat from the back of his neck and dabbed again at his throat. "If I should not survive my surgery—though I'm certainly not saying I expect that to be the outcome—I am willing to make you the beneficiary of my will. I will leave my entire estate to you—my house, my bank accounts, my various investments—if you will agree to do me one simple service."

"Let's hope you come through it just fine, and none of that matters."

"You and I have never been close, but we haven't been adversaries either, not as Marcella and I have been. But please don't suggest that my death would cause you great pain."

Ronnie didn't know what to say to that. And he stared at the clouds that had covered the sun, with an uneasy feeling in his chest.

"I want you to promise me in writing that you will prevent your Aunt Marcella from attending my funeral. I did ask my attorney to undertake the commission, but he claims he's unable to do so. He says a funeral is a public event, and he, as a member of the legal profession, can't be seen to interfere. That it would be far more appropriate for a 'quiet word' to be said from one family member to another rather than for an attorney to become publicly involved. Roger Trasker has never had what I would call intestinal fortitude, and I can now see I shouldn't be surprised."

"You want me to keep her from the funeral? Physically removing her if she showed up?" Ronnie was thinking about Dutton Harris. About the threat of losing his job. About what he'd inherit if cousin Sam died, and what life might be like if he were free to tell Harris what he could do with his job. Then his breath came shallow and short and he felt blood pound at his throat.

"Yes, exactly that. Your mother and I, as you know, have no very close relationship, and though we've stood on opposite sides of more than one family conflict, I have no intention of making such a request of you in her regard. But your Aunt Marcella is a different proposition. She shall not be allowed to gloat over my casket or display her habitual hypocrisy."

Ronnie shoved his hands in his pockets and stared at Sam's sweating face.

"I would've thought your response would be an easy one."

"You know I try to keep my mouth shut and stay out of family arguments."

"Yes, though I would've—"

"I'm not close to Aunt Marcella, you know that. I understand exactly why you've been fightin' with her over the years. She's a very difficult woman. She's not what I'd call rational, and she can be real vindictive. And I do thank you so much for considering me the way you have. But could I think this over for a while? I hate to react real fast."

"I leave day after tomorrow, and my will needs to be finalized. Your hesitation is a disappointment. I need your answer now."

Ronnie Holmes took his hands out of his pockets and shoved his hair back against the wind, while he looked at the line of trees that edged the closest paddock. "Well, I guess I have to say I'm sorry, but I can't go as far as you'd like. I could tell her her presence would cause some awkwardness and some pain within the family, and I could ask her not to attend and try to talk her out of it, but I don't reckon I can see my way to physically forcin' her away. Maybe she wouldn't even want to come. And I expect you'll come through anyhow, and it won't be any big deal."

Sam Freemantle stared at Ronnie and his face flushed as his hands clenched, before he turned toward his car. "You're more witless than I thought. To throw away a significant inheritance to keep from hurting that bitch's feelings? I imagine your mother'll be as proud as can be of your kind and upstanding behavior. But will your wife? Struggling to feed your several children on the pittance you make here? You don't have the brains you were born with!"

He was in his car in another minute, backing out and hurrying away, while Ronnie stood and watched after him, wondering how he would tell Angie, and what she would say.

Wednesday, May 12th, 1965

It'd been extremely hard for Michael to maintain a normal, calm, everyday face when talking to Dutton and Webber Swede—who at least seemed to be avoiding him, which did help some.

The whole situation seemed surrealistic—that the person managing his family's clinic, working everyday directly for his mom, was doing things they knew were dishonest, and they kept putting up with it. Yes, they were hoping to get incontrovertible proof that would get his license taken away, or at least get him censored by the Jockey Club. But having him there when they knew what he was was driving Michael crazy. And now having no doubt that he'd been behind the break-in made biding his time, and looking for the next move, a lot more difficult to do.

And then, Tuesday the 11th, Dutton had come looking for him to ask him to assist him with a surgery on a backyard horse near Paris the next day. He'd said he was a young colt with a scrotal hernia and he needed Michael's help during the procedure.

It made sense that he'd need help. Scrotal hernias, where the intestines slip through the inguinal canal into the scrotum, are serious and difficult to repair. They often lead to irreversible colic, and require more than two hands. They'd be operating on the ground at the farm too, with the colt sedated, and they'd have to work fast as well as carefully before the sedation wore off.

And yet why was Dutton asking him instead of Jerry?

It was out of character, certainly the last few months. Especially if they'd connected Glenn to him, which Dutton must've done. True, Jerry had calls scheduled that afternoon, but why did Dutton not ask Michael to switch with him and use Jerry instead? And they might need another person too to help position the horse.

When it came time to leave for the farm, the only additional hands that were free turned out to be Ronnie's, who did help with surgeries from time to time, and there wasn't any choice that afternoon. But Dutton looked anything but pleased when they were packing their trucks in the lot and Ronnie was climbing into Michael's.

Dutton chose a section of the lawn by the barn where the grass was thick and reasonably clean. And while Michael held the colt's halter, Dutton injected sedative into the big bay's jugular vein. The colt wavered and then collapsed, and Michael held his head and neck down till he was completely sedated.

The colt was lying on his right side, and Ronnie and Michael tied ropes to all four legs, while Dutton laid out two sterilized cloth wraps with scalpels and an ecrasure, as well as sutures and clamps, plus bandages and antiseptics, on the right side of the colt.

Dutton knelt beside them, as Michael stood on the colt's left and took hold of the rope attached to that rear leg. Ronnie picked up the rope on the right rear leg, while the owner and one of his sons grabbed the ropes on the front legs—and then, on the count of three, they all moved together to position the colt on his back.

Dutton had opened both wraps of instruments and selected a scalpel from the larger wrap, which held the ecrasure too, and made the incision by the hernia. Michael had knelt on the colt's left, and he pushed the intestines back into place and held them there so Dutton could castrate the colt and suture the inguinal rings properly closed to keep the intestines from falling again.

Michael had to lean over by Dutton so that their hands were positioned right next to each other's. And after Dutton had selected a smaller scalpel, his hand seemed to falter, and he stabbed Michael in the muscle on the outside edge of his left hand through his surgical glove.

Dutton said, "I'm sorry, Michael! I don't know how I did that! You okay to carry on?"

"Just tape a bandage across it, and I'll put on another pair of gloves."

The rest of the surgery went well. The intestines were sutured in place, the castration went without a hitch, and the colt got back on his feet, hanging his head and looking mildly confused, with no bad reaction to the sedative.

Michael cleaned the stab wound the way he normally would and didn't give it a whole lot of thought. It was the kind of thing that does happen when you're working

together in a tight space. And what would be the point of
Dutton doing it deliberately?

The next five or six days were unusually busy. There
were more emergency surgeries at the clinic than normal,
and there were a whole lot of everyday cases on the
outlying farms, and Michael began to feel like he hadn't
slept in a week.

And then he woke up, aching everywhere, with a
terrible headache, with nausea too, and a high fever, and
he had no choice but to call in sick.

He stayed in bed that day and the next, and Laura
came to make sure he drank enough water and ate
something when he felt like it, and Meg came when
Laura couldn't. The boy down the road took care of the
horses the way he always did when Michael needed him.
And Michael figured it was flu. A bad case but typical.
And he went back to work on the third day and tried to
keep his distance from everyone so no one else got
infected.

It took almost a week for him to feel normal, and he
was fine for three or four days before he began to notice
his urine looked darker than usual, and the headache and
fever came back.

Thursday, May 27th, 1965

Meg didn't get an answer when she phoned Michael at

home at ten o'clock that night, when she knew he wasn't working and wasn't out with Laura.

She had a key to his house, and she found him in bed with a high fever and a horrible headache. He was nauseated again, and his hands and feet were cold, and he lay there, with his eyes closed, trying not to shiver. His muscles and joints ached everywhere, and he couldn't get dressed without help when she said she was taking him to the hospital right that very minute.

He didn't argue the way he normally would, and that told Meg he knew how sick he was.

She put Wolf in the car, and called Laura from St. Joe's Hospital in Lexington, and Laura got there from Midway half an hour later, while they were still waiting for a doctor to see him, though they'd at least gotten him into a bed in a cubicle in the ER.

The ER doctor admitted him to a private room, after he'd asked a whole slew of questions, and a nurse had hooked Michael to a saline IV. The doctor said he was ordering tests, and they drew blood as soon they'd settled him into a private room.

The ER doctor told Meg and Laura that Michael would be seen by an internist in the morning, and they could come back during morning visiting hours—that he was sure they'd get to the bottom of it when they got the results of the tests.

Meg said, "I think he looks a little jaundiced. And his neck is stiff, he told me that, and you can see how exhausted he is. He's normally nothing like that."

Michael said, "Go home. Get some rest. We'll know

more tomorrow. I'll be fine. I'm better off here than at home. Please." He closed his eyes and pulled the sheet and blanket up under his chin and shut away the world.

Laura didn't want to leave any more than Meg did, but the hospital enforced its visiting hours, and the two walked out together.

Laura said she'd take off work and be back in the morning, and Meg told her she'd keep Wolf at her house and see her then.

Meg sat in her car for a minute, her hands gripping the wheel, worry freezing her heart the way it had years before. She could see Michael in front of her then, when he'd first started elementary school, when he'd suddenly begun having nightmares. His teacher, whom Meg knew from church, had called to tell her there was a bully in class who was tormenting everyone he could, and that it seemed to bother Michael especially, even when it was someone else the bully was attacking.

Then the nightmares stopped, as suddenly as they'd started—and the teacher called back. Michael had grabbed the kid out at recess and given him a good pounding, and though she'd had to discipline Michael, the bully was now behaving better, and Michael seemed to be fine.

Meg had suffered all through that week, wishing there'd been something she could do, even though she knew very well that you can't fight your children's battles.

This was another she couldn't fight for Michael. And she shuddered and closed her eyes and let out a long sigh.

"Don't let me lose him. Please. Not Missy, and Cliff, and Michael too. Take away the anxiety, Lord, and give me your peace the way you have before, because you know I've got none of my own."

CHAPTER TEN

Friday, May 28th, 1965

Neither the X-rays nor the blood tests told them what they'd hoped. They'd decided by late that Friday afternoon that it looked as though Michael had meningitis, even though they couldn't find bacteria in his blood that gave them a clear diagnosis or a way forward for treatment. They put him in an isolation ward, and everyone who knew Michael, and felt so inclined, began to pray that he'd live.

His fever was dangerous. His head and neck and back were excruciating. His kidneys weren't functioning the way they should—when the specialists at St. Joe's went off for the weekend.

They'd decided, though, before they left to let Meg and Laura into Michael's room if they wore gowns and masks. If they'd found bacteria in his blood, they wouldn't have. But because they hadn't, and were essentially baffled, they eventually agreed to let Meg and Laura in.

They were there whenever they were allowed to be, though most other hours of the day they either sat huddled together, or stranded in silent isolation, in uncomfortable chairs in a dingy waiting room with other families as worried as they were.

There weren't too many stretches of time when one of those strangers wouldn't break down in one way or another, and Meg, who wouldn't let herself, didn't know where to look. She'd get up and step into the hall to give the others time alone, and Laura usually came with her. The two of them would just walk up and down without saying more than a word.

Monday, May 31st, 1965

Laura saw Michael before Meg did that morning, lying silent in his tiny room with the one wide observation window facing the nurses' station.

It was hard for him to talk—to concentrate and find the energy to say much—even though he seemed to listen and understand what she said. He did give her a message for Meg, and she passed it on, standing in the hall, outside the waiting room door.

Laura pulled off her mask and cap, and her shoulder-length caramel hair seemed to spring away from her pale pinched face as though it had a life of its own. She pulled off her gloves and gown and leaned against the wall looking as tired as Meg felt. "Michael wanted me to tell you to take his research to your house. He says you'll know where to find it. He doesn't want you to keep coming in at night. He says it's too long a day. That you should go home, and walk the dogs, and try to get some rest."

Laura's hazel eyes were sad and shuttered, even when she tried to smile, and muscles were knotting along her jaw as though she were gritting her teeth. "He told *me* to go back to work and only come see him at night. That there's nothing I can do to help, and I need to think about something else besides what's wrong with him."

"Are you going to?"

"If I'm not here I worry more."

"He's right about the dogs. They need to get out and run. How did he seem?"

"Worse. I think. It's harder for him to talk. He ended up saying 'Dutton' a couple of times, but he never explained what he meant. They won't let you in now. They're giving him a sponge bath and doing some more tests."

Meg was studying Laura, seeing how much thinner she looked, how strained and tense and carefully controlled. "Why don't we walk outside for a while and get away from the waiting room. Unless you're going to work."

"I won't today. Will you come in tonight?"

"For as long as they'll let me. I just wish there were something I could do that might help."

They turned toward the elevators, both of them

walking slowly, as the doors slid open with a loud ping, and a family of four, looking stunned and disoriented, rushed out without even noticing that anyone else was there.

Once the doors had closed behind Meg and Laura, and there was quiet up and down the hall, Dutton Harris stepped out of the men's room, just across from the elevators, with a carefully neutral expression on the elegant bones of his face.

Ronnie showed up on his lunch hour asking to see Michael, but because he wasn't family the nurses wouldn't let him in.

The doctors knew no more than they had.

And Michael got steadily worse.

Meg and Laura tried not to discourage each other through the rest of the afternoon. Then Meg went home to take the dogs out. And Laura stayed on, trying to come up with something to tell Michael that had nothing to do with death and dying and pain that was hard to bear.

Tuesday, June 1st, 1965

Ronnie took the morning off and explained to Meg— once he'd found her in the hospital cafeteria, staring at a cup of coffee that looked like poisonous pond scum—

that there were things he had to tell Michael that might
help them figure out what Michael was fighting.

He didn't give her details of any kind, but she hunted
down every single doctor who had anything to do with
the case, telling them the same thing—sometimes
sounding determined but discreet, other times with
blunt-edged aggression—"You haven't discovered what's
caused his meningitis, if, in fact, he has meningitis, and
Michael may have a better perspective. He's a veterinarian. He knows the animals and diseases he's been
exposed to, and this young man thinks he has information that might help Michael come to some conclusion."

Finally, a little after noon, Ronnie walked into
Michael's dimly lit cubicle in a white gown and mask and
cap. He stood by the bed for a minute, staring at Michael
with worry racing through him, as Michael lay silent
with his eyes closed, saline dripping in one arm, a
catheter attached to a half-filled bag of unhealthy looking
urine, a flush on his sunken face.

"It's me, Michael. Ronnie. You gotta wake up now.
I got things I need to tell ya."

The fourth time he said that, Michael's eyes finally
opened, and Ronnie could see them searching the room,
trying to follow the voice.

"Can ya hear me okay? Can I tell ya some stuff and
you'll be able to understand? I don't know what shape
you're in, and I—"

"Have to talk... slowly."

"Dutton stabbed your hand, remember?"

Michael was trying to focus his eyes, trying to see who was talking behind the high white mask. "Ronnie?"

"Yeah. When Dutton stabbed your hand he took that scalpel from a sterile wrap that had nothing else in it. There was room in the other wrap for it, but the one he stuck you with was all by itself, and that's real suspicious."

"So…" Michael looked as though he were struggling to think, slowly and painfully, his eyes half-open again, but fixed still on Ronnie. "Say that again."

Ronnie did. Twice. Until Michael nodded.

"I'm thinkin' it could've been contaminated. Contaminated deliberately."

Michael moved his head from one side to the other as though the pain was nearly overwhelming, though his hot-looking, red-rimmed eyes bored even harder into Ronnie's.

"Another thing. There were three petri dishes in the small incubator with no identification on the lids. They weren't on normal agar, either. Two looked like they were on one kinda medium, and one looked like somethin' else. Nobody I talked to knew anything about them, and then after we did the surgery on that colt, that time when you got stabbed, the petri dishes disappeared."

"Crank my… head up." Michael seemed to be trying to scrunch himself higher on his pillows too, when he finally said, "Water," in a whisper. His lips were cracked and dry looking and his throat sounded parched when he spoke.

Ronnie turned the handle at the end of the bed till

Michael was almost sitting straight up, then held the glass with the straw for Michael, who stared at him without blinking for half a minute while he kneaded the back of his neck.

"I don't know nothin' 'bout what coulda been on that scalpel, but you started gettin' sick a week or so later, and I figure—"

"Mare... with aborted foal... Dutton's patient... before the colt."

"What farm? Do ya know?"

"No... Get the medical report."

"I'll be back as fast as I can."

"Get a doctor... now... not a nurse... Doc who's in charge."

When the doctor came in three hours later, Michael was shaking with fever and couldn't remember why he'd wanted him, once they woke him up.

Wednesday, June 2nd, 1965

Ronnie came back on his lunch hour and talked until Michael opened his eyes.

"It's me. Ronnie. Can you hear me?"

"Yeah..." Michael was searching again, looking for the face behind the voice.

"There *was* a mare with an aborted foal. Dutton mentioned it to Jerry at the time, and we figured out

what farm, but the medical report he filed says nothin'
'bout the foal being anything outta the ordinary. Just an
everyday miscarriage with nothin' peculiar about it. The
owners weren't home to ask. And I don't know what it
would mean that—"

"Get a doc... Stay while I talk to him... Tell 'em it's
an emergency."

It was almost an hour before Dr. William Reynolds, a
staff doc at St. Joseph's—short and thin and probably not
forty, capped and gowned and masked—stood next to
Michael's narrow bed, his eyes looking like he'd already
decided he needed to humor somebody.

Michael asked Ronnie to crank his bed up again,
while he tried to keep himself from shaking. Then he
turned his head toward Reynolds, as though his neck
didn't want to cooperate, and stared at the hooded eyes
hiding above the mask. "Leptospirosis... Won't be
bacteria in my blood now... Exposed too long ago."

"The chances of it being leptospirosis—"

"Bacteria was put in a wound in my hand... fluids
from an aborted foal... aborted because of lepto... timing's
exactly right... Flu... then fine... then meningitis
symptoms."

"Why would you think—"

"*Listen to me!*" Michael pulled the doctor down, his
hand like a vise on his upper arm, the doctor's face inches
from his own, his chest almost against Reynolds's,
breathing his hot sickly smelling breath into the doctor's

mask. "Bloodborne. Not airborne… Don't need masks… Bacteria was cultured from fluids from organs in the infected foal… Maybe urine. Maybe liver… Get me on penicillin G! Intravenous! Now! … Then look for lepto antibodies."

"So this was the result of a lab accident?"

Michael let go of Reynolds's arm. His own fell hard across his chest, and he seemed to be struggling to take in enough air, his face red and contorted, his eyes closing before he said, "Ronnie… make him start penicillin G… Tell Meg now."

When Meg talked to Ronnie, when she saw clearly for the first time what Dutton had actually done, she told Ronnie not to say a word to anyone anywhere about what they'd found. Nothing about the scalpel, or the leptospirosis, or the bacteria being cultured—nothing. And he had to keep Jerry from mentioning anything about the aborted foal. They couldn't prove lepto came from the scalpel. Or that Dutton had cultured the bacteria. And she didn't want to decide what to do before she could talk to Michael when he was more himself.

It was almost two hours before they got the penicillin going, and Michael slept most of that, but then he'd talked to Laura, when she came in at four from work, and he explained to her that he'd be all right. That the penicillin would knock out the bacteria. He told her not to tell anyone what was wrong with him or that he'd recover. Let them assume it was hopeless.

"Why?"

"I want to be in my right mind… when I deal with Dutton."

She was trying to tell him what a relief that was, and what the thought of losing him had done to her, when a nurse came in and asked her to leave so she could treat the patient. Then Laura did what Michael had asked her to do—she went on home to get some rest and go to work the next day.

Meg called the clinic while Laura was in with Michael to tell Ronnie again how grateful she was for what he'd done—noticing, and thinking it all out, and saving Michael's life.

She asked if Jerry had said anything about the foal to anyone, and Ronnie said he swore he hadn't and surely wouldn't now.

Meg got the name and address of the folks who'd owned the foal. Then thanked him one more time and hung up the pay phone in the hospital lobby. She took the elevator up to see Michael whenever the nurse was done.

"How do you know it's leptospirosis?"

"Symptoms and timing… Flu… week after I was stabbed… Okay, a few days… then meningitis symptoms.

… Could've been kidney failure… or bleeding in the lungs… lepto can cause it all."

"You're sure you'll be all right?" Meg was standing, hugging her arms against her ribs, tears standing in her eyes.

"Yeah… I will… after a while."

"What do we do, Michael? Dutton Harris tried to kill you."

"Let him figure I'm dying… Give me time to get better. You read about lepto…"

"I'll study it this afternoon. We know so much of what he's done and can't prove hardly a thing."

Michael nodded, but didn't say anything. He just lay and rubbed his neck.

It was six o'clock when Meg rechained the gate at the Metzgers' farm and drove to the barn in back. It wasn't far from the road—maybe two hundred feet—and it was a small barn, in poor repair, with a rusty horse trailer parked off to one side.

Meg parked next to it, and walked around to the east end of the barn, once she'd heard talking inside.

A man and wife, probably in their early eighties, both white-haired and stocky—the woman filling water buckets for the two horses that were watching her from their big clean stalls, the man about to toss flakes of hay over their half-doors.

Meg introduced herself and asked if she could speak to them once they'd finished their chores.

"Sure. Just give us a minute. I'm Rhoda Metzger. This is my husband Wes." She disappeared inside the feed room dragging the hose behind her.

"So what can we do for you?" Wesley Metzger looked at Meg shyly before he picked up a push broom.

"I've retired as office manager of my husband's clinic, but I still help out, and we've discovered that some of our records are missing. You had a visit from Dr. Harris back in April, and I'm wondering if you have your copy of his report so we can update your file."

Wes Metzger swept bits of hay and straw from the aisleway into an empty stall, then hung the broom on the wall. "I don't reckon we kept the copy, but I can tell ya what happened. Rhoda here can too. Our mare, Tess, she was in foal, and everything seemed just fine, and then come April she lost the foal."

Meg said, "I'm sorry. I've lost foals myself."

"Harris come out and saw to her, and did an autopsy on the foal right here, taking some samples of the liver and the like, and urine from the bladder and all, and said he figured it coulda been a disease. Somethin' that gets passed on from rodents. From their urine, and from horse urine too, from an infected animal, getting in the water. Maybe puddles out in the paddock where a horse'll drink. We've scrubbed out the stalls real good, and we've spread the manure pile on a hayfield out back. And done every-thin' else we could."

"Did Dr. Harris examine Tess to see if there was anything wrong with her? Thinking she'd passed some-thing on to the foal?"

"He checked all her vitals and all. Nothin' real extensive."

"Had she had any symptoms? Anything like moon blindness?"

"She did have a spell of that back in late January, or maybe early February. But that went away quite a few weeks before she lost the foal. Dr. Harris knew that. We called him out when it happened."

"We're not gonna get Tess in foal again." Rhoda Metzger poured a scoop of grain in Tess's feed bucket, then went back in the feed room to get one for the gelding. "We're not getting any younger, and we don't want her to go through losin' another. Or us, come to that. Walter, the gelding here, he's been fine. No signs that he's been sick."

Meg said, "It couldn't've been easy, with the autopsy and all."

Rhoda nodded, and Wes shrugged and shoved his hands in his pockets.

Meg didn't say anything more for a minute. She just watched Walter start in on his grain and thought about what to say. "Did Dr. Harris treat Tess when he was here the time she lost the foal? Or come back later and treat her in anyway?"

Wes said, "Nope."

And Meg nodded, then turned toward Rhoda and Wes. "Would you be willing to write out what happened during that visit, and sign your names so it's official, and then I can get it back in the file?"

Wesley said, "We can do that. If you wantta wait. We've had supper, and there's nothin' on TV."

"Why didn't ya ask Dr. Harris to fill out another report?" Rhoda was watching Meg with more than curiosity. She was looking like she smelled a rat but was too polite to say so.

Which meant Meg had to answer the question she'd been hoping to avoid. "He's been really busy, and I was driving by tonight and decided to stop on the spur of the moment."

Rhoda looked Meg in the eye and said, "That don't make much sense."

"My husband and I started this practice, and I'm responsible for keeping it going so that every vet that works for us does what my husband would think was right. I'm trying to make sure every horse is treated the way it should be."

Rhoda stared at her a minute. Then nodded and said, "Come on inside, and we'll write you out what happened."

Meg got back to her cabin at seven thirty, and put on tennis shoes and an old pair of slacks. She was hungry, but the dogs were ready to get out, and she took their leashes and let them out the French doors on the west side of the sitting room. She started across the lawn behind her cabin, walking slowly, rubbing her right hip, leading them across the hill and down toward the woods that edged a deep ravine above a wide shallow creek.

They walked over to the drop off, then through the

woods on a riding trail, before starting down the long lane that led between the paddocks to Jo and Alan's house.

Every so often Meg's eyes would glaze over, and she wouldn't notice what the dogs were doing. She'd be thinking about leptospirosis, and what she'd read that afternoon. That they think it causes recurrent uveitis, or moon blindness in horses, that comes and goes over time. *Which means Dutton knew what was wrong with that foal, and that's why he took the samples.*

"Wolf! Jessie! Come when you're called. It's time to go in."

It was eight thirty when they got back, and Meg went into the kitchen to see what she could put together for some kind of supper. There wasn't much but eggs and cheese and mushrooms, and two early tomatoes Toss had brought from his garden. She made herself a mushroom omelet, arranged it on a dinner plate, and sliced a tomato on another.

She'd just sat down at her oval table by the east window in the sitting room, when she saw Jo and Emmy walking down the lane toward her door.

"Come on in, Jo. I'm in the living room."

Wolf and Jessie were both escorting Jo, one on either side, as she talked to them, coming through the kitchen, carrying a manila envelope and a small basket of strawberries. "I left Emmy outside. I thought it might be too much having three of them in here."

"No, bring her in. Or let them all out. That's an idea. She'll keep them where they should be."

Jo did let them out, and then she sat opposite Meg, who asked if she'd like an iced tea.

"No thanks. I'm fine. My friend Buddy brought me this on his way home tonight. It's from the groom Michael talked to. Buddy's friend who works up in Louisville? He didn't know Michael's address, and heard he was sick anyway, so he drove it over to Buddy. You weren't home earlier, so Buddy handed it to me."

"I never would've thought that he—" Meg could feel her heart hitting harder and her face beginning to feel warm. She opened the envelope and took out a letter-sized envelope that was addressed in capital letters to Mr. Michael MacInnes.

She tore the flap and pulled out five sheets of blue-lined notebook paper, the top one a letter in longhand.

Dear Mr. MacInnes,

I been thinking about when we met at my cousins house and I reckon I did wrong. I acted in a cowardly fashion. I did not stand up for what I knowed to be right. Dutton Harris and the fellow that worked for him, and Ray Black the owner of Night Captain, they all did murder and I let them get away with it for fear my family would be harmed. I will do better now. I have wrote down what happened on that plane, the date and everything so it can be checked. My wife and my brother signed the last page two so everyone will know it was me that wrote it down.

Yours very sincerely
Tate Smalls

Meg handed Jo the letter, then read the other four pages. She pushed them across the table to Jo, and then held her napkin to her mouth. Her face seemed to freeze for a second, while she raised her right hand as though she were asking Jo to give her a minute. She took a sip of tea, then dropped her hands in her lap. "Harris tried to kill Michael."

She told Jo all of it, for almost an hour, going over every bit of information and how it had come to them, with Jo asking questions and looking more and more concerned.

"Michael will be alright. It may take awhile, and his kidneys may never be quite the way they were. But we aren't telling anybody that. We're trying to figure out what to do that will trap Dutton into doing something drastic that we can actually catch him at."

"That sounds risky. Especially now."

"I imagine it is, but what else can we do?"

"You here alone. With Michael still sick." Jo was staring at Meg, wondering how a self-contained lady in her late seventies could be sitting there calmly talking about murder, and how to stop the killer.

"I don't see any other choice. It's coming to a head."

"I wish it wasn't now."

"You mean right now, in particular?"

"Alan and I have to go to Schenectady for two weeks. His dad had a heart attack last Saturday. I didn't want to tell you when you had everything else on your mind. They say it was a mild one and that he's doing well, but Alan wants to spend time with him and talk to the doctor too. I don't like thinking you'll be here alone with no one else on the property at night. Toss will be here during the day, and sometimes at night, if he's expecting a mare to foal any time soon. But Spencer won't be in the tenant house. He's going to be away this coming week to meet the cousins, or the aunts or something, of the woman he's been dating."

"I've got Wolf and Jessie. And I'm not unarmed." Meg smiled.

And Jo laughed. And then didn't see much reason to. "I could ask Toss to move into our house, if you think—"

"No, Jo. I'll be fine. Just pray I'll come up with a plan. Something I can carry out before Dutton finds out Michael's on the mend."

"One thing I meant to tell you before, when you were spending so much time at the hospital. There's an old fenced-in dog run that comes out of that shed past our house that you can always use if you need to leave the dogs for longer than you'd want to leave them inside. They could get in and out of the shed and stay out of the weather."

"Thank you. I don't know that I'd need it, but it's good to know it's there."

"We're taking Emmy with us. Alan's folks want to see her, and we can't leave her here on her own."

"I could take care of her if—"

"No, you couldn't. You've got enough to worry about without another dog."

CHAPTER ELEVEN

Thursday, June 3rd, 1965

At nine that morning Meg read Michael her typed copy of Tate Small's account of Harris killing Night Captain. She'd put the original in her safe, and brought a copy of Tate's covering letter as well, and read that to Michael too.

"That took courage… for him to take the risk."

Meg smiled and said, "It did. And yet there's no hard and fast proof."

Michael nodded, while he reached for his glass of water.

Meg leaned over and handed it to him and waited while he drank. "Tate *knows* his coffee was drugged, but there's surely no way to prove it now."

"The licensing authorities can't ignore the letter… can they?… When we give them other evidence?"

"Except—"

"We've got nothing concrete."

"How are you feeling?"

"Headache's better."

"Your color looks more normal."

"So... when they find the leptospirosis antibodies... they'll take me out of isolation... If Dutton phones to ask my condition, he'll know I'm getting better."

"Which means—"

"That I figured out what he did."

"I see."

"That could make him attack. In some way. To keep us from taking action against him... I don't want you in the cabin with Jo and Alan gone."

"I've got the evidence in the safe, so he can't get his hands on that. And Dutton would have a hard time getting past Wolf."

"Maybe."

"I b'lieve dogs know when a person means you harm."

"That's not enough, Ma... It's not."

"Well, we'll have to give it some thought."

"Have they tried to break in to my house?... You'd think with what they did at Glenn's—"

"Nothing that I've seen. And I've stopped there most days to pick up your mail. If I don't, Laura does, and she hasn't said anything, and I feel sure she'd notice. Am I wearing you out? You're looking more tired than you were."

"I'm tired. Not like I was." Michael grinned for the first time in weeks.

And Meg smiled back inside the mask they were still

making her wear. "I'm going to pick up last month's accounts at the clinic so I can go over them this afternoon. I'll tell everybody you're worse, but I have to get away from the hospital for a while and think about something else, though I'll surely come back here tonight."

"You don't have to. Laura'll be here. You take some time for yourself."

"We'll see. Have her call me if she can't."

"Did I thank Ronnie?" Michael smiled again.

And Meg took off her surgical gloves and slid one hand down his cheek.

It started raining about seven that night, and a quick burst of hail pelted down half an hour later. Meg ran out when it slackened off and drove her car into the old storage shed between her cabin and the barn where Jo kept Sam. Jo had told her she could use it as a garage, but she hadn't seen any reason to until the hail hit.

It pounded the ground again half an hour later, ripping branches and stripping off leaves, battering the cedar shake roof—some the size of ping-pong balls, some the size of popcorn, bouncing when they hit the lawn, a foot or two in the air.

It lasted fifteen minutes, while Meg played two Bach preludes, and Wolf and Jessie lay and listened, probably to the fury of the storm, while they looked out the south window without even beginning to panic the way a lot of dogs would.

Meg hadn't bothered to turn on any lights, and when she got up from the piano, she sank into the old velvet chair by that south window and sat in the dark of the storm, listening to the thunder and lightning, watching it electrify the sky, feeling her body begin to relax—the shoulders first, and the sides of her neck that were still as hard as iron to the touch from all the days of worry—and thought about going to bed early. About taking a long hot shower and sliding between her clean soft sheets, trying to sleep all through the night for the first time in weeks.

Then Wolf shot straight up off the floor, barking loud enough to shake the walls—making Jessie jump up after him, barking and snarling and following fast as he flew down the two shallow stairs into the long east hall.

Wolf threw himself against the glass door, three times or maybe four, barking as though he were demented, Jessie snapping beside him—both of them with their hair up the whole length of their bodies—as Meg stood stunned by the stairs.

A second later they sprinted through the kitchen, lunging, then, at the French doors in the living room, barking and snapping and growling—till they stopped and stood and listened—then shot back through the hall, up the steps past Meg, to the cabin's old front door on the other side of the piano.

Wolf stood straight up on his back legs and clawed the wood with his front nails, while they both barked and growled for another minute—before they stood, still and listening, as though they could hear whatever threat it was retreating into the storm.

Meg rushed into her bedroom and stood to one side of the east window, where she looked out, hidden in the dark, and saw Dutton Harris in his Barbour raincoat, carrying some kind of satchel, hurrying toward the pickup that was parked at the curve of the lane, just past the shed where she'd shut up her car.

Meg froze there, hardly breathing, straining to see through the rain and the dark, with Wolf and Jessie, their hair still up, growling low in their throats.

She waited till she saw Dutton turn on his headlights —suddenly, slicing into the dark, down the lane past Jo's. And then she took one long deep breath before she turned from the window. "Wolf was a very good boy, and Jessie was very good too, and we need to go get you a treat."

Wolf followed Meg into the kitchen, but left the piece of cheese in her hand for the first time in his life, and circled the house again—east door, to French doors, to old front door in the music room—sniffing the cracks at the bottom where each door met the floor, his fur still up and his big ears cocked, his ice-blue eyes hunting prey.

"It's okay, Wolf. He's gone now. You don't have to worry anymore."

He looked at Meg and sat for a minute. Then trotted back to the kitchen and stared straight at the counter where she'd left his piece of cheese.

She patted them both and rubbed their ears. And

then walked back to her bedroom where she swiveled the overstuffed chair by the fireplace till it faced the narrow window.

It was still raining at eleven o'clock, slower then, and softer, and Meg could hear horses in Sam's barn whinny before she saw the lights go on, as Toss, who'd come from his house near Versailles, to check on all the horses he'd kept in, in every one of Jo's barns, because of the storm.

Meg was still up at midnight, lying in bed then, with her knees bent, staring at the wood plank ceiling, Wolf and Jessie on their beds beside hers, one of them snoring gently.

He had to have been after the evidence. That's why he brought a satchel. And risked coming early too when he thought I'd still be at St. Joe's.

Michael was right. He's looking for a way to try to stop us. Even though he doesn't know Michael's getting better, or what evidence we have.

And here I am, old and on my own. At much too much of a loss.

I know what needs to be done. I simply don't know how to go about it. I have to create a situation that forces Dutton to do something illegal that gives us enough evidence we can call the police.

I s'ppose it could be breaking and entering.

Or attempted murder, that would be better.

Though I'd like to avoid an actual death. Especially my own.

Meg smiled then and tucked her hands underneath her head, her gray hair spread across the pillow, while she stretched her legs the length of the bed.

If he thinks Michael's dead, and that I've got the evidence Michael gathered against him—especially if he thinks I've got something more incriminating than anything I do have—if he thinks I'm the only one who knows about it, then he'd be likely to try to stop me. Though whatever trap I come up with has to be set, and put into effect too, before Michael's moved.

And yet, for Dutton to come assault me now, he'd have to think the dogs aren't here, or be prepared to kill them both while he tries to get in.

What would provoke him to try to attack me before he knows Michael's better?

Whatever I come up with, I can't let Michael know. He's not strong enough to lie there alone fretting about me.

Probably the first thing I need to find out is Dutton's schedule for tomorrow. Perhaps the next day too, depending. And then I have to decide who I can truly count on without Jo and Alan.

Ridgeway Rockwell for anything legal.

And Ronnie'll back me up at the clinic.

Though with what, remains to be seen.

Close your eyes and pray like your mother did.

Then relax every one of your muscles and try to get some sleep.

Friday, June 4th, 1965

Meg called the clinic at eight that morning and asked to talk to Ronnie, but Eliza, who'd answered the phone, wondered if she could speak to her first.

"Certainly. Now would be just fine."

"There's something I feel like I oughtta mention. Dr. Harris came in here just after seven and asked me what happened to the safe you used to have in your office. I told him you took it home when you retired. I said I thought it'd belonged to you before you started up the business. I don't know why he wanted to know, and I hope I did right to tell him what I did."

"That was fine, Eliza. Exactly right. Thank you for letting me know."

"Good. I wasn't sure I should've. I'll connect you to Ronnie right quick."

"One other thing while I have you on the phone. What's Dr. Harris's schedule for this afternoon?"

Meg got to the clinic at four thirty, accompanied by a locksmith, who went right to work changing the locks on the front door.

As Dutton walked into reception, after having finished with the clinic cases for the afternoon, Meg told Eliza that with all she was going through, she'd taken Michael's dog, and her own dog too, to a kennel for the night so she'd have one less thing to worry about. "Last night while I was gone they about tore the place apart during that hailstorm, and with everything I'm having to face, I feel like I need a break."

"If there's anything that I can do to help, you know I'd be happy to. I'm so sorry about Michael."

"Thank you, Eliza. I appreciate that. Could I talk to you for a minute, Dutton?"

"Of course! Let's step into my office. What's the repairman doing with the hardware?"

"I'll tell you in just a minute."

Dutton laid his hand between Meg's shoulder blades and guided her through his door.

She sat in one of his guest chairs and set her briefcase on the floor.

He settled himself and smiled across at her while he folded his hands on the desk. "It's good to see you, Meg. How's Michael doing?"

Meg opened her briefcase and pulled out a sheet of Ridgeway Russell's letterhead and laid the document on the leather desk pad right in front of Dutton.

He looked at her silently for a second, before he picked up the letter addressed to him at the clinic.

June 4, 1965
Dear Dr. Harris:

According to the terms of your employment contract with MacInnes Equine Veterinary Services, dated September 12, 1963, your employment is duly terminated, without stated cause, today, June 4, 1965, by the majority shareholder, Margaret Elger MacInnes.

You will remove your belongings from the clinic

forthwith, and leave your keys to the facility and to the
clinic vehicle with Mrs. MacInnes before your immediate
departure.

Sincerely,
Ridgeway Russell, Esq.

"Meg—"

"Michael died this afternoon. He knew you infected him with leptospirosis, but he discovered it too late. You cultured it, and smeared it on the scalpel you stuck in his hand.

"I know Night Captain shouldn't have been killed. I know about you stealing semen from successful studs and doing artificial insemination. I know you blackmailed Dr. Madden and drove him to kill himself. I have evidence of that, and much else. And I *shall* be taking this further.

"I don't know if I can prove you murdered Michael, but I'm certainly going to try. I'll put the materials I have before the Woodford County sheriff, as well as the Veterinary Licensing Board, and the Jockey Club too. I intend to drum you out of the profession at the very least, if I can't put you behind bars. I haven't revealed what I know yet to anyone else. I've been too preoccupied with Michael. But I shall be able to now."

Dutton stood and stared down at Meg, his face rigid and his eyes on fire, his hands clenched at his sides. "You don't know what you're saying. I didn't do anything to Michael. How can you think that? Grief is making you irrational."

"You never even bothered to treat the mare who had the aborted foal."

"What's the significance of that? She can be treated anytime. Night Captain went berserk. Madden was a weak-kneed, incompetent—"

Meg stood then, shaking slightly, and picked up her briefcase. She opened the door to the front hall and called to Ronnie, who was waiting down the hall in reception.

He ran up and held the door and waited for Meg to walk through.

"The locks are being changed now. Ronnie and I will stand here and wait for you to empty your desk, and then he will escort you off the premises. Eliza will call you a taxi."

"If you think that I—"

"Don't speak to Mrs. MacInnes in that tone of voice." Ronnie was bristling, his arms out away from his sides, his jaw set hard, the look in his eyes the one he'd earned slogging through mud in Korea.

Harris glanced at Ronnie, and then looked at Meg, and sat down in his chair. "You're making a terrible mistake. Who do you think can run this practice without me? Jerry? Jerry's the reason I was brought in. You have the right to terminate me, but it won't be long till you regret it."

He opened his center drawer and began setting his belongings in the middle of his desk. He moved on to the side drawers, but before he'd finished emptying them, he glanced at Meg without any expression and reached up to a reference book on the shelf beside his desk. He pulled out a sheet of folded notepaper and slipped it into the side pocket of his coat before he gazed at her and smiled.

Meg had taken the dogs to Jo's kennel before she did what she had to do to get ready for Dutton. She'd tried to make herself eat dinner, but she'd just sat and stared at the table, going over and over what could go wrong. Asking whether he'd come or he wouldn't. And if she had the courage to do what she thought would have to be done.

Mostly since then she'd been walking the cabin in loose slacks and a shirt with rolled up sleeves under an old safari vest Cliff had had for years. The last hour she'd been looking out her bedroom windows, the lights off except in the kitchen—till ten minutes after ten when she saw a shape in the dark walking across the riding area behind Sam's barn.

She hurried up the stairs to her office, as fast as she could without tripping, and started the tape recorder she'd set in a cardboard box on a shelf beside her desk.

She was down again, in the music room, when she heard the knock on the east door.

She turned on the hall light, and the light outside on the shed-roofed porch beyond the wide glass door, but she didn't see anyone when she looked out.

She knew he had to be there. Off to one side, where she couldn't see him, and she opened the door and said, "Toss is that you? I didn't think you were coming tonight."

Dutton Harris rushed at her from the left side of the

door, wrenching it wide with gloved hands. He shoved her back with his right, while he stuck a hypodermic against her right arm with his left hand. He pushed her back across the hall till he'd bent her backwards over the top of the mahogany chest next to the bathroom door, saying, "Tell me where the safe is!"

"You aren't going to inject that. You need me to unlock the safe."

"Where!"

"Upstairs in my office."

He half dragged her up the U-shaped stairs, the needle pricking her skin, as she limped up, trying to hold the railing to keep from losing her balance.

They turned left when they stepped off the stairs toward where the desk stood under the east window, and the safe sat straight in front of them against the wall to the right of the desk. It was tucked under a shelf lined with old cameras, next to two on tripods on its right—and as Harris pushed her down on her knees and watched as she entered the combination, the needle still pressed against her arm, he said, "Why so many cameras?"

"They're the one thing Cliff collected."

"And you can't part with anything of his. I bet you've still got his medical bag in a sacred spot in your bedroom." Harris said it like an insult.

And Meg didn't answer him back while she tried to stand up.

"No, down! Pull everything out and put it on top of the safe."

Meg did, one file and envelope at a time, trying to

keep her right arm from pushing against the needle. "What's in the hypodermic?"

"What do you think I'd use?"

"Chloral hydrate, probably."

"Good for you! But then your husband was a vet. Up. Stand against the other wall." He still held the hypodermic against her as he pulled her up and pushed her across to the bookcase on the side wall opposite the safe and the cameras.

Then he stepped back and took a folded note-sized sheet of paper from his inside jacket pocket. He laid it on the left end of the desk, then pulled out a small brown bottle sealed with a metal and gray-rubber top and set it beside the paper.

"What's written on the paper?"

"This?" Dutton Harris picked it up and smiled. "'It's gotten to be too painful. I can't deny the truth any longer, and I know Cliff would agree. I can't go on. I know I can't, in my heart and my mind too. Wishing it were different doesn't make it so.'"

"I wrote that to Michael when I gave up riding my horse. There was another page, about giving my horse to a good friend, and giving him Cliff's before I moved, and asking him—"

"He used it as a bookmark and forgot all about it. And, of course, Michael isn't here to say it isn't a suicide note."

He smiled then, and backed toward the safe, and set the hypodermic on that end of the desk. He transferred the files from the safe to the desk, still keeping an eye on

Meg, even when he opened the files. "So. Pictures of me doing AI. Negatives too, that's good. I can say I'm injecting an antibiotic, and nobody can prove any different."

He looked at the information Michael had gathered on Proper Introduction's "breedings" first, and Watcher's too, and the other stallions Michael had uncovered—with the letters Michael had gotten folks to write, along with Cliff's notes—and he smiled and set them on the desk.

"So let's see what you've got on Night Captain." He glanced through Tate Smalls' account. And shook his head at Meg. "For crying out loud, it's the groom! An uneducated Negro hot walker who doesn't know what he's seen. It's two against one, with Swede Webber and me telling our side of the story. So that won't hold up any better than the AI accusations. If Smalls had pocketed the cup with the sedative, then it might've been different."

Dutton took a nylon bag with a zipper from his coat and smoothed it out on the desk. He slid the papers he'd looked at inside, then picked up Anna Madden's letter describing how he'd blackmailed her husband. "Nothing here but a secondhand account, and a great deal of supposition, plus inconclusive bank statements that won't support your case." He slipped it all into the nylon bag and picked up Ronnie's letter.

"So Ronnie saw the cultures. He didn't take samples and send them to an independent lab. He can't prove what was in those petri dishes, or if I put anything on the scalpel. I assume it was Michael who came to the conclusion I'd used leptospirosis."

Harris was staring intently at Meg, and she nodded, but didn't answer. "You can't even prove the foal was infected. Even with the letter from the owners. She was, of course. And I can't tell you how glad I was when the foal aborted. I saw right then that I could culture fluids from the fetus to kill Michael in such a way that not one doctor in a thousand might hope to have a clue. If this were a third world country it would've been different, but—"

Harris glanced through the other papers, looking at Meg every few seconds, shoving one paper after another into the bag on the desk. "Nothing else is significant. The suggestions that I didn't do work on farms that I charged for. Or falsified medical reports for sales, or the track, or injected a diuretic at Keeneland. None of that can be proven, or is any real threat."

He shoved the rest of the files in the bag. Then zipped it up and laid it on the desk again, before he turned to gaze at Meg with pale, half-dead eyes. "You, on the other hand, are an intractable threat. You won't drop this. You'll do as much damage as you can, even without the documents."

"Those weren't the only prints Glenn made. And the people who testified against you will be only too happy to do it again." Her back was to the bookshelves, her eyes fixed on Harris, her left hand gripping the spine of a hardback she'd pulled to the front of the shelf.

"Yes, I suppose they will. And you won't hesitate to

ask them." He picked up the hypodermic and started across to Meg.

She'd taken a step off to her right and had turned so she was facing the desk at an angle, when he grabbed her left arm and shoved the hypodermic toward her right.

She threw the book on the floor hard, and less than a second later they heard the shutter of the Nikon on the closest tripod click once—then three more times.

Harris spun toward the camera, the hypodermic still in his hand, as Meg took three steps away from him and pulled her snub-nosed .38 revolver out of a pocket in her vest.

"You know I know how to shoot. And I promise you I won't hesitate now!" She backed up again as she spoke, till there were eight feet or more between them.

"Oh, yeah!" He was grinning at her, looking as though he were trying not to laugh. "Target practice isn't the same as shooting a living person. You think you could do it, old lady? You think you could stand there and put a bullet in my chest in cold blood?"

Meg backed further away from him and yelled, "Glenn!" before Dutton laughed.

They were ten feet apart when Dutton lunged at her, and she shot him in the left thigh. He stumbled and grabbed his leg and made a noise deep in his chest Meg would never forget.

But it didn't stop him, not the way she'd thought it would, and she shot him through the upper right arm just below the shoulder.

The shots sounded like an artillery burst in that thick-walled log cabin, and she backed away again, yelling at him to stay where he was, but he took one more step toward her and she shot him again in the same leg, and watched him go down.

He dropped the hypodermic, screaming and swearing.

And she stood still, with her heart thundering in the hollow below her throat, as she listened to Glenn Cook limp up the stairs carrying his own 9mm handgun.

She swallowed against the dryness in her mouth, watching Dutton writhe on the floor, then took a deep breath and let it out slowly, trying to control her heart. "Michael's alive. They've found the antibodies. He'll be out of isolation tomorrow."

CHAPTER TWELVE

It was three o'clock in the morning before the ambulance and the county sheriff and his two deputies had left Meg and Glenn alone.

Meg handed Glenn a bottle of Cliff's Burgundy and asked him to pour them both a glass while she drove down to Jo's and got Wolf and Jessie out of the shed with the dog run.

The two of them ran around the outside of the house three or four times, then sniffed every room, concentrating longest where there'd been blood in the office, before they lay down in the living room next to Meg's feet.

She'd eased herself down into the high-backed chair between the fireplace and the French doors, sore everywhere from being pulled and pushed and shoved onto her knees, while Glenn sat on her end of the sofa and set his left foot on the coffee table so his leg was stretched straight out.

They sat in silence for a long time, the last of the

adrenaline seeping away, leaving them frayed and exhausted.

"I didn't expect it, but it might've been the hardest thing I ever had to do." Glenn was rubbing his thigh inside the brace, his wine untouched on the table.

"What?" Meg's blue eyes were dull and tired-looking when she turned to Glenn, her fingers tight on her glass.

"Listening to what Dutton was doing to you. Waiting downstairs till you dropped a book. Or made some other kind of loud noise so I'd know to take the pictures."

"Do you see any other way we could've done it?"

Glenn didn't say anything. He arched his eyebrows contemplatively above his large hazel eyes, but his jaw muscles were knotted and his lips looked pinched and tense.

"You know he had to think he and I were alone."

"I know. And I had to listen to what he said from the bedroom, but—"

"And you couldn't have taken the pictures the way you did if you hadn't stayed there."

"They'd better come out is all I've got to say! I used fast film, and there should've been enough light, but I won't be able to relax till I see the prints. You'd think the police lab would be good at developing negatives, but I don't know if we can count on it."

"I didn't expect the sheriff to be as interested in the camera as he was." Meg smiled then, as she remembered Earl Peabody—the tall, broad, big man in a brown-and-tan uniform, his huge hands on his hips—leaning over

the tripod, looking at the hole Glenn had drilled in the
floor.

"It's the first camera he's seen that has a motor drive."

"I don't know what that is."

"It advances the film so you don't have to do it man-
ually. That's why I could be downstairs and push the
button on the cable and get more than one shot."

Meg nodded and sipped her wine, then crossed her
arms across her chest.

"You realize how close we came to not being able to
pull it off? If your office floor hadn't been your bedroom
ceiling, I never could've snaked the shutter cable through."

"And you know without your father's cameras the
Nikon would've stuck out just like a sore thumb. You
think Dutton's attorney will say we set a trap, and that—"

"Even if he does, I don't believe a judge or a jury
here in Woodford County will fall for that kind of non-
sense. They'll see Dutton was trying to kill you, just like
he tried to kill Michael, and they'll use some common
sense."

"I hope." Meg smiled with worry underneath it, as
Wolf whimpered somewhere in his chest and his legs
twitched in his sleep. "I truly hope the legal procedures
won't take months. The thought of becoming a public
spectacle the way Alan and Jo did last year—" Meg shook
her head, then stared at the empty hearth.

"You'll come through it just fine."

"I will. I expect. God willing." Meg was quiet then,
sipping her Burgundy, staring past the dining table at the
darkness beyond. "I surely never imagined myself shoot-

ing another person. That's the crux of what troubles me
most. Yet I can't see I had any other choice, no matter
how I look at it."

"You didn't."

"And now, being investigated because of that—"

"The sheriff said it'll be a formality. With everything
we've got on tape, and with—"

"I hope so. Though whether or not they'll allow the
tape to be used as evidence remains to be seen."

"I *heard* Dutton admit everything he did. That makes
it two against one, even without the tape the sheriff took
from the recorder. We have pictures too, pulled right out
of the camera, also by the sheriff himself, developed by
the police lab."

"Courts don't always decide on what's true, or fair,
or makes good sense."

"No, but it's as good a system as we've got."

"True." Meg brushed her hair back from her face and
glanced across at Glenn. "Nothing made by man ever
gets close to perfect."

"No, it certainly doesn't."

"Ridgeway Russell'll tell us more tomorrow, so that'll
be good."

"It will. Though the evidence seems to me to be
nearly incontrovertible. Michael will testify too. And
Ronnie. And what they know will help. That was very
good wine." He put his empty glass on the coffee table
and set his hands on his thighs.

"I'll go see Michael first thing in the morning. I don't
want him to hear a word from anybody else."

They were both silent again then, reliving it all one more time, even after having gone through it more times than they could remember with Earl Peabody and his deputies.

Glenn said, "We'll have to go to the sheriff's office to sign our statements too, probably by early afternoon."

"I couldn't remember what time he said."

"I'm sleeping on this sofa, by the way, for what's left of the night."

"I'll be fine, Glenn. You don't have to—"

"I'm not leaving you alone tonight. There needs to be somebody here." Glenn smiled at Meg, then leaned down and stroked Jessie's head.

"Thank you. I appreciate everything you've done so much." She swallowed the last of her Burgundy and set the glass on the coffee table next to Glenn's.

She was quiet then, and when Glenn looked over, there were two tears sliding down her cheeks, and her lips were pulled in tight together as though she were trying not to make a sound.

Excerpt for Jo Grant Munro's Journal
Thursday, December 2nd, 1965

I've hardly touched my journal since Dutton was arrested, and I can't say I understand why. There've been six months of stress, and strain, and public scrutiny for Meg and Michael, and maybe that's part of it. Alan and I know what that's like. And I hope that talking to us has helped them make their way through it.

I think it's been worse for Meg than for Michael. Her generation finds it harder, even than Michael's and mine, to discuss feelings and private matters with folks on the outside. And with Meg being her own sort of introvert too, having her private fears and most intimate trials picked apart by the public must be nearly unbearable. Especially without Cliff to come home to. Alan and I had each other last year, and that made a definite difference.

At least Meg was cleared of the shooting not too many days after it happened. Having to protect herself was traumatic to begin with, and going through the legal process was almost as alarming.

Dutton recuperated as well as anyone could've. He may not be a contender for the hundred-yard dash anytime soon, but he did okay. He didn't even need a bone graft.

They took him to St. Joseph's Hospital (ironically, while Michael was still there), where they kept him under guard for two or three weeks before they took him to the Woodford County jail. Fortunately for the rest of the world, they've kept him there ever since. Earl viewed him as a flight risk, especially once they'd found the coins and cash and watch collection in the safe at his house. The prosecutor agreed with Earl, as did the judge, so he didn't get out on bail.

Michael got back to work a month after Dutton was arrested, weaker than he'd been before and with headaches he hadn't had previously, but he's gotten better since then. He took over the practice too, even though he would've rather had a few more years working under someone like his dad. The first thing he did was fire Webber Swede. The second thing was rehire Nancy Petrosky.

Meg went back to work there even before he did, so she could take some of the administrative stuff off Michael's shoulders. She doesn't intend to stay, but they're understaffed with only two vets, and she can pick up some of the slack. They're hoping to hire another vet, but with the revelations in the press of the kind of treatment Dutton gave his patients, they've lost a number of clients. That, and probably the fact that while Michael was still sick, and Dutton was gone too, Jerry couldn't keep up with the work.

Sometime right in there, Nancy Petrosky's sister Marie died of what they think was bleeding in the brain. I suspect it came as some kind of release, but it left a hole in Nancy's heart too that probably won't be healing up soon.

Michael and Laura got married in September (with twenty family and friends in attendance) in Meg's backyard at the cabin. The weather was perfect. Esther Wilkes, Charlie Smalls's sister, catered the food, and it couldn't have been better. Dutton's trial started November 3rd, and he was convicted on two counts of attempted murder today at four o'clock. The sentencing will take place tomorrow at eleven, and I've arranged for a babysitter so I can take Meg. I know she's afraid he'll get off too easily, and end up hurting someone else the way he did them.

Friday, December 3rd, 1965

Dutton Harris was sentenced at 11:30 a.m. to twenty years under Kentucky law for two counts of attempted murder, and was transferred immediately to the Kentucky

State Penitentiary in Eddyville, while his mother sat in the front row and cried, straight backed in her chair, a handkerchief hiding her face.

Meg and Michael talked quietly for a minute in a back hall in the courthouse, with their heads close together, while Laura and Jo and Ronnie and Glenn stood a little way off and gave them time to be alone. Michael hugged her and kissed her on the forehead, then motioned the others over.

Meg thanked them all for everything they'd done to help, and then she announced she was taking the afternoon off. "I am so bone tired I have to go home and lie down. It seemed like I was struck down as soon as I heard the sentence." She laughed then.

And the others smiled—and went their own ways.

Jo drove Meg home in her pickup to help Meg elude the press and the bystanders, both of them talking a blue streak, and dropped her off at the cabin.

Meg ate cheese and crackers and a large orange, and then took off everything but her underwear and slid between her sheets.

It was three o'clock when she heard the knock on her door. Jessie dashed out of the bedroom and clattered down the music room stairs, while Meg made herself get out of bed and look out her bedroom window.

A black Cadillac sedan with Virginia plates was parked next to her Dodge.

She stood where she was for a second, tempted to take the coward's way out and refuse to answer the door.

But she smoothed her hair back toward her chignon, pulled on the cream-colored blouse and tan tweed skirt she'd worn to court, slid her arms into the matching jacket, and eased herself down the shallow steps into the east hall.

Dutton's mother stood on the other side of the wide glass door, just as Meg had known she would be, in a black wool suit and white silk blouse, a large black purse clasped in both her hands.

Meg told Jessie to sit. Then took a deep breath and let it out again, before she opened the door.

Meg had laid a wood fire in the living room the day before, and she lit the newspaper under the kindling on her way to hand Elizabeth Harris a cup of coffee with cream.

Mrs. Harris had seated herself on the sofa where Glenn had sat all those months before, and Meg settled next to her, into her highbacked overstuffed chair, stiffening herself for whatever Dutton's mother had come from Lexington to say.

"I'm sorry to bother you, but I felt as though I had to come and tell you how sorry I am for all you've been through."

Meg couldn't think of anything she ought to say to that, and she warmed her hands on her coffee mug and stared straight at the fire.

"It seems so unreal." Elizabeth Harris sipped her coffee, then set the cup and saucer on the coffee table. She was still the kind of woman you notice, even though she was in her mid-sixties, with dark hair streaked with silver framing gray eyes in a fine-boned face, with a trim, athletic-looking body beautifully dressed in classic clothes. And yet even so, she didn't give the impression of being overly concerned with how she looked—not like women who've invested their lives in making men notice. "Still, I do have to say, I find it hard to believe that Dutton did all those horrible things, though—"

"The prosecution presented a case that certainly convinced the jury."

"I'm sorry. I didn't express myself very well. I do accept the evidence. I do believe he did those things, but it's come as a terrible shock. He was such a good boy when he was little. He was kind to every animal he—"

"Was he?" Meg said it as though she wanted to say more but had the good taste not to.

"I thought he'd make a fine veterinarian. His father never cared for horses, but Dutton started riding with me when he was only three."

Meg didn't say anything. She nodded and sipped her coffee.

"Dutton's father was a difficult man. He was very attached to money, and inherited position as well. His family had lost a great deal of both in the Depression, and that affected him profoundly."

Meg wanted to say they weren't the only ones hurt

by the Depression, but she got up and threw another log on the fire before either of them spoke.

"Willard was terribly hard on Dutton, though I never fully understood why. He criticized him no matter what he did, and never made him feel as though he were loved or respected. I believe that must've been very difficult for an intelligent, sensitive boy."

"A lot of folks have grown up with fathers who've been a good bit more difficult than that."

"And then, of course, when his father was found to have done something terribly dishonest in his law practice, it set Dutton a very poor example. Willard never did seem to feel remorse, and I believe that affected Dutton adversely."

"How did you treat Dutton?"

"I tried my best to compensate for his father's lack of affection."

"When you saw him getting hurt by his father, it must've been a real temptation to justify whatever Dutton did."

"You mean did I minimize, or explain away actions of his that weren't proper?"

"Yes. Do you think he felt you treated him in such a way that you'd overlook whatever he did, even if it were wrong?"

The delicate face looked startled for a second. And then she shook her head. "I certainly didn't perceive it that way, no. I expect I tried to put a positive interpretation on much of what he did, in order to encourage him, but—"

"How has he treated you? Has he stayed in touch and been—"

"Dutton has always been very committed to his career. And with the hours a vet has to put in, I didn't expect him to come home very often. I knew he had a life of his own, and I didn't wish to interfere." Mrs. Harris picked up her cup and stirred her coffee, then set her spoon in the saucer.

Neither of them said anything else for a minute. Meg knew exactly what she wanted to say, but told herself it wouldn't help.

"You and your son, Michael, seem to be very close."

"I think we are. Thank God. He's the only family I have left. My husband and I lost our daughter during the Second World War."

"Sharing an interest in the clinic must be a bond. An enterprise that engages you both and helps to keep you close."

"It does. Yes. Though the responsibility can be daunting. There are larger clinics here in central Kentucky that have been in business much longer than we have and can afford more sophisticated equipment. With Michael ill, and my husband gone, and the controversy around the recent treatment of the horses in our care, it'll be increasingly difficult for us to compete. We're also understaffed, and Michael's newly qualified. Ideally, we would have a senior vet to mentor Michael for a few more years before he takes over, but the way things have turned out, that won't be possible for a while yet. At least as it looks now."

"No." Elizabeth Harris glanced at Meg, then looked away quickly as her face crumbled in upon itself, and she began to cry as though nothing anyone could do would help.

Meg couldn't think of anything to say, and she stared at the fire until Dutton's mother blew her nose and worked at drying her eyes.

"I'm sorry. I told myself not to burden you with my situation."

"I'm sorry it's so hard on you."

"Was it me? Am I responsible for what he's become?" Her red-rimmed eyes were begging Meg for some kind of denial, or a word that would let her go on.

"No. Dutton made himself who he is now. With one choice after another."

"I've loved him so much, all his life, and I don't think he's ever cared for me, not one little bit!" She looked appalled then—as she set her cup and saucer down and sat forward on the sofa. "That's a terrible thing for me to say. I don't mean that at all. I'm sure he loves me very much, but it's never been easy for Dutton to show his deepest feelings."

They were both silent for a minute before Meg drank the last of her coffee and looked directly at Elizabeth Harris. "Being a parent's the hardest job I've ever had. I know one thing I tried to do, consciously, with both our children, was, first of all, be truly consistent myself, and then make them admit it when they'd done something wrong. That's much easier for some parents than it is for

others. It's a little like training a dog." Meg laughed then
and smoothed her skirt farther over her knees.

"I don't know that I—" Mrs. Harris was silent for a
minute, pulling at her handkerchief with both her hands.
"I know this might not be the right time. With everything you've gone through, with Michael having been so
ill for so long, but I believe it might make a very great
difference for Dutton's future, when he comes up for
parole and all, if you were to write the authorities and
support an appeal for clemency. Even now, if you could
find it in your heart, so it would be there in his file. I
know that's a great deal to ask, but as a mother, knowing
how you would feel if that were Michael there in prison,
I thought you might be willing." She glanced at Meg,
and then looked away, as though she were half-ashamed.

Meg leaned over and stroked Jessie's back, waiting for
help and insight, trying to collect herself before she said a
word. Half a minute later she turned sideways in her
chair and looked at Elizabeth Harris. "I watched my son
die by inches, day after day, because Dutton Harris
wanted him dead. And I'm far more concerned about
what Dutton would do to someone else, if he were to be
released, than I am for him in prison. I'm sorry, but he
shouldn't ever be in a position again to injure an innocent person—or a helpless horse, either one."

Elizabeth Harris didn't say anything else. She nodded
and tried to smile. Then she picked her purse up off the
floor and walked through the kitchen into the long hall
and out the door to her car.

CHAPTER THIRTEEN

Friday, April 8th, 1966

They'd been inside and outside too, in Glenn's living room and his library-dining room, on the screened-in porch and the kitchen, in the backyard and the front yard—but not in the studio. He'd had a lock put on that door, and he'd decided to use it with guests in the house.

They'd come that evening, after the opening of his one-man show at the Keeneland Clubhouse, so he could thank them for showing interest in his work. The spring races would start the next day, and his show would last through both weeks of racing and not close until after he'd finished two talks on the history of equine painting in England and America.

The one regrettable blot on the evening had occurred because Samuel Freemantle had come to the exhibit—not because he was the least bit interested in art in general, or Glenn's work in particular, but because, as an accountant working for Keeneland, he'd thought he'd detected pressure from above to attend every race-week event.

Apparently, Marcella, who was still furious with Ronnie, knew Ronnie would be there and decided to attend on her own. The harangue that escalated between Sam and Marcella was already beginning to get out of hand when Ronnie and Michael escorted them both outside, where the Keeneland security folks made sure they departed the premises.

What made it worse for Glenn was that it was an honor to have Keeneland offer him a one-man show, especially during the races, when people would be there from all over the world. He was still stunned, and frazzled too, after designing and mounting the show, while he'd hurried to finish a couple of new paintings and make arrangements with owners to loan others so he could put together a comprehensive group that showed the range of his work. Having it disrupted by the Freemantles had been a real embarrassment.

But now, as he leaned against the archway into his library-dining room, his back to the front hall, he grinned at Jo as she walked through the last of the family and friends to bring him a glass of champagne.

"It went very well. You put the show together beautifully."

"Thanks. Except for Sam and Marcella."

"Nobody blames you for that, and it's not worth worrying about now. You know, I watched Meg and Michael in front of Cliff's portrait before anyone else got there, and it almost hurt to see how much that painting matters to them. They've had it for months, but even so it—"

"Painting it was important to me. I owe them a whole lot."

"The reverse could be said as well." Jo's dark-brown hair was swept up in back, swirled sideways somehow so instead of being a chignon, the ends curled loose on one side, making her look both elegant and casual in the scooped-neck, black-silk cocktail dress she wore for special occasions. "What you did for Meg with Dutton has not gone unappreciated."

Glenn smiled and sipped his champagne, but didn't look at Jo. "It helped me as much as it did Meg and Michael." He waited for a minute and considered his words as though saying what he wanted to say was not going to be easy. "After I was hurt, when my fiancée decamped, and I had to give up riding, it changed the way I saw myself. The ex-military, athletic horseman had exited overnight."

"But you're still in great shape. You lift weights and swim like Alan does, and you—"

"But if someone near me were attacked on the street, and I wanted to help, I couldn't the way I once could have."

"Maybe, but—"

"I did something useful for Meg in a crisis. And that was good for me too. By the way, this house works so well for me—when I'm here alone, or with two or three others, and for all these folks tonight. Thank you."

"I really enjoyed doing it." Jo could see Glenn didn't want to say more about himself, anymore than she wanted to be complimented on her work, and she changed the subject again. "I thought that friend of your sister's, the art teacher, whatever her name is, is an interesting person. And she really likes your work."

Glenn looked at Jo and laughed. "I didn't figure you for a matchmaker. You're not the first to point that out."

"No?" Jo laughed and put her arm around Alan's waist when he walked over, limping a little the way he always did from a wound he'd taken in France.

"I really enjoyed your show. And you can count on us coming to your talks." Alan was four inches taller than Glenn, six-four barefooted, but they were both strong and broad shouldered and had grown up serious about their work—and they'd always been easy with each other.

"Thanks. Having two people in the audience will be much better than none. You know, Ronnie was telling me that the Woodford County Historical Museum is doing its first special exhibit on the woman who was murdered here and the confession we found in the wall. His cousin, Sam, is hopping mad and trying to make them cancel it, and the cousin he's always fighting with, she's trying to get on the news again so she can rub it in."

"While Ronnie and his mom try to ignore the whole thing. Typical." Jo said, "Hey, Michael. How are you doing? How's the clinic?" when Michael and Laura walked over, Laura carrying a tray of celery with shrimp dip the caterer had brought from the kitchen.

"Better. My advisor at the UK vet school has agreed to work as a consultant, so that's been good. And I've been going out to see Dad's old clients to explain what happened with Dutton, and what we're trying to do now. It's had some pretty good results so far, so I'm hoping over time things will begin to turn around."

"What about you, Laura? How's your work at Keeneland?" Jo set her champagne glass on a bookshelf then turned back to Laura.

"At the moment, I'm trying to introduce the Thoroughbred library to as broad an audience as possible. It's a very extensive archival collection that was started in 1936, and people all over the world can benefit from what they've put together, so that's been fun for me. And finally living in the same house with Michael has been more than entertaining." She laughed then and hugged him, and he kissed the top of her head. "Wolf seems to like having extra company too."

"Wolf would. The only time I've ever known him to take against anybody was that night at Mom's with Dutton. Where is Mom? Has anyone seen her?"

"Alan and I are driving her home, so she hasn't left. Last I saw her she was on the back porch."

Michael walked through the kitchen, chatting with the caterer, and on out through the open door to the screened-in porch.

Meg was there, sitting in a wicker chair, side-lit by the light from the kitchen, staring straight ahead past the candles in hurricane lamps that edged the back of the porch.

"Hey." Michael said it quietly as he stepped toward her chair.

"Hey, yourself."

"What are you doing all alone?" He sat in the chair that backed up to the kitchen so he could see her face.

"You know me. I don't do well in crowds for very long."

"Most everybody's left."

"It's been sounding like maybe they had." Meg took off her round gold earrings and slipped them in her purse, then rubbed both her earlobes as though they'd begun to hurt. "I was remembering your dad after Missy died, when he decided to quit his job and start his own clinic. Seeing Glenn's portrait in the exhibit—I don't know why, when we've had it at the cabin—but it brought back a whole lot of memories I haven't thought of in years. We had a very good time together working on the business."

"I know you did. I got to watch."

They were quiet then, in a swirl of night sounds, of insects and laughter and the clatter of dishes and good-byes getting said.

"You're a strong old lady. Some might even say tough."

"Am I?" Meg smiled, then looked away and laid her hands in her lap.

"Your last year, watching the clinic crumble. Seeing me in intensive care—"

"I didn't go through it alone. You, and Ronnie, and Jo, and Glenn. Tate Smalls, and all the rest, they all helped. And I do believe we were being looked after the whole way along."

"Yeah, I think we were."

"You saw Dutton destroying your dad's work with your own eyes every day. That was worse than hearing about it. And being as sick as you were, that must've been—" She reached over and patted his knee and let the silence settle. "I'm glad you're my son. And that you've got Laura."

"Yep. Me too."

"You know how I record my practicing when I'm working on a difficult piano piece?"

"Yeah."

"I'm thinking about making a tape of what it was like, being without Cliff to consult with, learning what Dutton was doing to you and the clinic. I figure it'll help me to describe how it felt. Watching you become so ill. Confronting him at the house. I'm still dreaming about it. All sorts of bits and pieces of it, some real and some not. I can talk to Jo, and you know I can talk to you, but there's more I want to get down for me. And now with Dutton's lawyer starting in with the appeals and all, I need to do something more to put it in perspective."

"I dream about it too. When I'm not so busy I fall asleep in my soup."

"Another thing I've been thinking about. I believe I'm going to ask Jo to design me a little house some-where. I was thinking I might want to live in Midway. I could walk to the post office, and the drug store, and a restaurant when I don't want to cook, and be close to Dr. Fisher."

"You're not sick, are you?"

"No. No, thank God. And I'm not in any rush. I really enjoy living in the cabin and being out in the country, but I'm getting old, Michael. Being someplace closer to town, I believe it makes good sense."

"Just don't do anything in a rush. I'll be able to buy a place one day, and you could have a parcel to build on."

"You don't need to start your married life with your mother next door."

"If you were a different kind of mother, I wouldn't. But you being who you are, I'm not worried."

"Don't speak for Laura. She might be appalled."

"She's not. Getting to know you when I was sick was one good thing that came out of the whole disgusting mess."

"I appreciate you saying that. I do. And I would miss Jo if I moved. Though we'd stay close, wherever I live."

"Yeah, I'm sure you would."

"Another thing I'm thinking is that I should start teaching piano to folks who can't afford lessons. Being around children again would be good for me—and for them too, I hope. Being in a village would make that a great deal easier to accomplish."

"You've been making an awful lotta plans."

"I have to. I can't let my life stand still right here with what happened with Dutton."

"You'll have grandchildren of your own, you know, barring some—"

"I know. I hope I do."

"Meg? Are you about ready to go home?" Jo was standing in the kitchen doorway, looking from Meg to Michael. "I didn't mean to interrupt."

"No, not at all. Yes, ma'am, I am." Meg pushed herself out of her chair, just as Michael stood up. She put her arm through his, and they started toward the door. "Why don't you bring Emmy over tomorrow? Jessie could use a good run."

"I'll bring Ross too. Jessie can herd both of them to her heart's content."

"I'm trying to teach her not to wind herself around your legs the way she does, but a herding dog's stubborn." Meg laughed and patted Michael on the shoulder as she walked toward Glenn to say goodbye and make arrangements to pick up Cliff's portrait when the show at Keeneland was over.

THE WIRE

Glenn Cook married the art teacher who was a friend of his sister's, and they had a daughter and a son shortly thereafter—which meant they needed an addition built onto Glenn's house. They're both grown now, with children of their own. And Glenn's about to retire from the faculty of the fine art department at the University of Kentucky, where he's taught, while doing his own work, since the late 1960s.

I did design a house for Meg in Midway—a small, one-story clapboard with a few large rooms—that I think she came to love. She walked around town, as long and as far as she could, with Jessie, and then another dog, Jack, until he died, making friends with neighbors and shop owners, watching the world with interest and insight, while doing what she could for those she came to know who needed what she could give.

She moved in in 1969 when she'd just turned eighty and her first grandchild was one. She loved Alex and the two girls who came next, but she wasn't a pushover. She made them behave when they were with her, while she read to them and taught them to cook and took them on walks as long as she could, back out at our farm with all the horses and foals and dogs that came along over the years.

Meg died in her sleep in 1980 when she was ninety-one. She'd had some heart troubles in recent years, but it was as peaceful as anyone could've hoped. She didn't live to see her grandson, Alex, suffer through a car accident a few days after she died, which he ultimately recovered from, though it was a tough situation for him and his whole family.

Long before Meg died, there was a time when Dutton Harris gave everyone reason for concern again when a lawyer he'd found in Frankfort tried to institute a retrial. That failed, fortunately. And, of course, he worked to get early parole as well. But the time came, before that was determined, sometime in 1974, that Dutton died of prostate cancer while he was still in prison. None of us gloated—least of all Meg—but there were probably more than a few sighs of relief that he wouldn't ever be out in the world doing the things he did.

Michael was able to save the clinic, though there were long years of struggle and worry, that probably continue today, the way it is for most businesses as the world and the work changes.

Losing Meg was a loss for me as well as for Michael and Laura and their children. Meg was still learning, still teaching piano, still reading and working in her garden, until the day she died. She set me a very good example of what I hope to be able to do for as long as I'm given time.

Jo Grant Munro
December 1999
Rolling Ridge Farm
McCowan's Ferry Road
Versailles, Kentucky

ACKNOWLEDGMENTS

It was Peggy Brown—an internationally known clinician and Centered Riding instructor (American Riding Instructors Association's Instructor of the year in 2005, who attempted to teach me Centered Riding and has been a friend ever since)—who got me thinking about artificial insemination in Thoroughbreds and what that could lead to with a dishonest vet.

Susan E. Harris—also an internationally recognized clinician, riding instructor and equine author and artist (2004 Master Instructor for the American Riding Instructor Association and Peggy's associate in Anatomy in Motion)—has a deep understanding of the history of the horse industry in the US, and she gave me valuable assistance in thinking about the Thoroughbred industry and the way the equine world worked back in the sixties.

Still, most of the research I did had to do with equine medicine, Thoroughbred breeding and fertility in particular. I interviewed several equine vets (most of them in Kentucky) in order to grapple with equine medicine as it was in the midsixties. They were all very qualified, very interesting, and very helpful, but as you'd expect, there were differing answers to various questions, and I had to try to assimilate it all and choose the "right" answers. Which means whatever mistakes there are in *The Outsiding* are definitely my own.

The equine health industry has changed so enormously since the sixties that vets who are practicing today have a necessarily limited grasp of what it was like back then. But they helped. They went out of their way. They did research on my behalf and put me in touch with retired vets, because if I didn't find out what was possible back then, the plot wouldn't have worked. For instance: blood typing can determine a horse's parentage, and if they'd been able to do that in 1965, my primary premise wouldn't have held up.

It wasn't until someone (I unfortunately forget who) suggested I call Dr. Gus Cothran—a much published and respected equine geneticist at Texas A&M—that I got a definitive answer. He told me that Clyde Stormont at UC Davis had been the undisputed authority on equine blood typing and that it couldn't have been done in 1965. Dr. Stormont had written two papers on the subject in 1964, and a couple of universities might've been gearing up to try it in 1965, but no universities had perfected it, and no vet practices could've tackled it. Even in 1973, when Dr. Cothran started graduate school at UK, they kept a herd of sixty to seventy horses to be able to get the antibodies to make antigens to do the testing, which no clinic could've afforded.

But as usual, the vet I pestered most was Rick Martin, who cared for my horses years ago before he began to concentrate on small-animal work. He took care of Jake, our boxer dog, and he's a long-suffering source of all kinds of information. The most critical example is that the story depended on finding a lethal disease that can be transmitted from horses to people but was curable back in the sixties. Rick helped me research zoonotic diseases (those transmittable from animals to humans) and then evaluate my options.

I also knew I wanted the dishonest vet to stick someone with a scalpel that was contaminated with the bacteria (which meant the disease had to be bloodborne), and Rick suggested the scrotal hernia as an operation during which it would be easy for one vet to poke another, then described it for me in detail.

I eventually settled on leptospirosis, but there was much still to be worked out about timing and symptoms and whether introducing the bacteria in the hand would've put enough bacteria into the bloodstream to actually be deadly, and I got the information I needed from Rick, supplemented by others.

And, like all the other vets I talked to, Rick helped me imagine the kinds of unsavory practices a dishonest vet could've been involved in. He showed me the rod and syringe that are used to do AI, and put an ecrasure for gelding a horse right in my very own hand.

There was much else I needed to know too—sedatives used in the sixties, surgeries that a small clinic could have done then, how nerving and roar surgery and firing were done, how splintbone injuries would've been treated as well—and Rick Henninger from University Equine

Services at Findlay University in Findlay, Ohio (who cared for my last two horses), gave me hours of his time and helped with that and much else.

As did Johnny Mac Smith, an equine vet in Versailles, Kentucky, who works for the Grayson-Jockey Club Research Foundation, as well as Keeneland Racecourse evaluating X-rays of the horses being sold during their Thoroughbred sales.

We talked about sedatives and surgeries and equipment back then, portable X-rays in particular, and he told me about an insurance scam in Ocala, Florida, he came up against shortly after he'd qualified. Two partners owned a colt who needed a life-saving surgery on his ankle, which Johnny Mac's clinic duly performed. One of the horse's owners paid for the surgery, but the other partner hadn't wanted the horse to have it. He wanted him put down in order to collect the insurance. But the colt did well—till the second morning after surgery, when he was found lying comatose in the treatment barn.

They eventually figured out that during the night someone had come in—using only a match to light his activities (the spent match being later discovered), since turning on the lights would've alerted the night duty vet —and injected him with insulin. They got a viable blood sample that showed extremely low blood sugar, indicating an overdose of insulin, as well as the vein puncture from the injection when they did the autopsy. It later turned out there were a series of these deaths involving insurance fraud up and down the east coast being perpetrated by a small-animal vet.

That's what led me to have Dutton, in his musings at home, refer to that insulin overdose, wondering if Michael could've found out about it, even though the killing itself doesn't take place in the book.

Johnny Mac also put me in touch with Dr. Gary Lavin, who's a well-known vet in Louisville and Lexington (Distinguished Life Member of the American Association of Equine Practitioners; the recipient of the Kentucky Thoroughbred Owners 2014 Warner L. Jones Horseman of the Year Award), and who's very knowledgeable about equine medicine and the racing world in the midsixties. His father had been race secretary at Churchill Downs, and Dr. Lavin had spent many years there as well as a practitioner and surgeon.

He knew what drugs were available, and what surgeries could've been done, and what everything cost then. He knew a lot about what could've been falsified and how it would've been hidden, and was suitably appalled by the risks the occasional real-life vet will sometimes take even today by gambling on a race, which, if it's discovered, leads to losing your license. He'd had to work so hard to get through school and set himself up in business that the thought of risking his license for anything, much less a casual bet, was inconceivable to him.

Becky Ryder, library director of Keeneland Library, helped me in 2017 with a wide range of dates and facts. Betsy Baxter, since retired as library and archivist technician at Keeneland (who helped me earlier in all kinds of ways) put me in touch with Dr. Ed Fallon, now retired, the fourth generation of the Hagyard family to work as an equine vet at what's now called the Hagyard Equine Medical Institute, where his son carries on the tradition. He was very gracious and kind, but it was painful for him to even think about the sorts of dishonest things an equine vet might do.

Ms. Baxter also put me in touch with Ercel Ellis, the host of *Horse Tales*, a very popular radio talk show in Lexington, who, *Keeneland Magazine* says, "Delights fans week after week with homespun stories and interesting guests." Mr. Ellis has an absolutely encyclopedic knowledge of Thoroughbred genealogy and race statistics, as well as the human-interest particulars of trainers and jockeys and horses and owners throughout Thoroughbred history. He and I only talked by phone, but his anecdotal insights into Kentucky's horse world helped me a lot.

One of those sources—who shall remain nameless—did tell me of a rumor around town of a fine Thoroughbred stallion having been put down on a plane for no reason except to collect the insurance.

I spent hours at the Keeneland Library working through books and periodicals from the fifties and sixties I couldn't have found anywhere else (which is where I studied furosemide—the diuretic called Lasix today that's frequently prescribed now for Thoroughbreds when they race).

I read about a very successful vet in Louisville, now deceased, whose horses won an amazing number of stakes races, including those in the Triple Crown, who was followed and investigated and prosecuted too for questionably innovative practices as well as for using drugs that weren't legal for use in horses (though some of them are now). To say he was a colorful personality would be an understatement, and his contradictory character gave me a lot to think about.

I also read about Dr. Robert Copelan (an excellent vet and pioneering orthopedic surgeon, one of the founders of the American Association of Equine Practitioners) and learned a great deal from reading about him. I also found a physical description of the equine hospital at Sunnyside Farm he established in 1972 that allowed me to visualize what would've made sense for MacInnes Equine. I used that description to draw a floorplan I could work from that would reflect a reasonable size and level of sophistication for a clinic in the midsixties.

Keeneland Library has a wonderful collection of exceptionally fine equine art displayed on its paneled walls, which helped me consider styles and approaches for the equine painter in the plot. I particularly admire the work there of Quang Ho, whose paintings have also been used for the covers of more than one *Keeneland Magazine*. Much more art is tucked away in the library's archives, and Dan Prater, library assistant, very kindly took me behind the scenes to view that as well.

In addition to the vets and the librarians who helped me in Lexington, friends I've made in Woodford County while writing the Ben Reese *Watches Of The Night*, as well as the first two Jo Grant books, went out of their way too. Jonelle Fisher and her husband, Dr. Jack, answered a lot of questions about life there then and also took my husband and me to tour Old Friends, a non-profit home for retired racehorses (which figures directly in *The Outsiding*, as you'll see in the Historical Notes). Jonelle has written several books on the denizens of Woodford County, historical and contemporary, and in the Historical Notes I talk about how one of those books got me thinking about a particular part of the plot.

Jim Rouse, a very experienced, very gentlemanly lawyer in Versailles, helped again with legal questions, as he did for *Breeding Ground* and *Behind The Bonehouse*. It's his and his wife's farm I describe as Jo's and Alan's, and I've spent many idyllic hours there walking that ridge watching the mares and babies that belong to the trainers and owners who lease the Rouses' land.

As always, I loved being in Woodford County—meeting new people and talking with friends, doing the research that's always interesting. And as I've said with boring regularity, if the realities of our lives had been different, my husband and I would've moved there.

HISTORICAL NOTES

Watcher, the Thoroughbred stallion who didn't want to do anything he was told, including breed mares, is based on a real stallion I met one morning at Old Friends, a nonprofit retirement home for Thoroughbred race-horses in Georgetown, Kentucky, just north of Midway.

Old Friends was started by Michael Blowen and his wife, Diane, after they took early retirement from writing for the *Boston Globe*. Michael had written film criticism and met a whole lot of Hollywood folks, but he says he was never so starstruck as he is around the champions who're relaxing in retirement while he waits on them—Silver Charm (with whom I had an instant connection), along with Gulch and Touch Gold and too many others for me to name here—as well as the also-rans with characters and personalities that can make them at least as appealing.

Watcher is based on War Emblem, who won the Kentucky Derby and the Preakness in 2002 and stood a very good chance of winning the Belmont—or would have if he hadn't stumbled nearly to his knees coming out of the gate.

Bob Baffert had taken over his training that year and

was calling him Hannibal Lecter by then because of his penchant for biting any living creature who came near him. He'd act up in the gate, and would only race well if there were no horses in front of him, so when he stumbled in the Belmont coming out of the gate, and then bumped another horse, Baffert knew he wouldn't do squat with the field already in front of him. Even so, War Emblem actually did make a late move, though Baffert still says, "I had to sit there for two-and-a-half minutes and wait for the race to be over."

War Emblem was sold in 2002 to the Yoshida racing family in Japan for more than seventeen million dollars—but nothing changed. He wanted to do what he wanted to do. He had no use for mares (much the way he hates all gray horses) and getting him to breed was incredibly difficult and dangerous (and yes, he did do all the things to avoid it I say Watcher was guilty of). Still, of his 111 foals who raced (out of a total of one hundred and nineteen), 80 were winners, which is a very high percentage, and presumably made trying to get him to cooperate worth it. A group of equine psychologists from the University of Pennsylvania were flown over to work with him, and they did have some early success with small chestnut mares, but that didn't last, and in 2012 he bred only three mares, none of which became pregnant.

In 2015 the Yoshida family chose not to have him slaughtered (as many old racehorses sadly are), but to let him retire at Old Friends. Before he could set foot on the farm, however, like all stallions who've been bred abroad, he had to be quarantined for a month and breed two mares to prove he didn't carry contagious equine metritis. He was quarantined at the very prestigious Rood and Riddle Equine Hospital in Lexington, but he refused to breed even once, and he had to be gelded before he could be sent to Old Friends.

He'll now stand still and let Michael Blowen feed him carrots without trying to bite him, but everyone else has to be kept at a safe distance. Michael says he's the smartest horse he's ever met. Baffert says he would've been the leader of any wild herd—and who would argue with him?

Sarava, the horse who beat War Emblem in the Belmont, a 70-1 longshot who astonished everyone, is also at Old Friends. It'd be interesting to know if they recognize each other, and what they think if they do.

The story line in *The Outsiding* that has to do with the old murder that had taken place in the house Glenn is renovating is based on two real-life murders I read about in Jonelle Fisher's book, *Nantura*.

Nantura is the name of a horse farm that was owned by the Harper family, which John Harper (a well-known horse trainer in the mid-to-late 1800s) named after one of his mares, who'd done well on the track and later bred a long string of very successful runners.

John's brother William had married and had children, and then died young, earlier in the 1800s, leaving John and his brothers Adam and Jacob and their sister Betsy (none of whom ever chose to marry) to live together amicably in the family home. The four of them grew old together—Jacob running the farm; Adam lending money for a living; Betsy cooking and caring for the house; John breeding, training, and racing Thoroughbreds.

In November 1864, brother Adam was shot and killed by a marauding band of guerrillas who came to steal their horses—though they left, in the end, without them. Jake and John and Betsy, and the bloodlines John had bred, survived the rest of the Civil War and set about rebuilding their lives, working hard, living frugally, being charitable to their neighbors.

In September 1871 John took his famous horse, Longfellow, son of the mare Nantura, to Lexington to the track and stayed with him in his stall till morning in preparation for the first big race. In the darkest hour of the night, John heard someone rattling the door of the stall trying to get in, asking to see Longfellow. John refused to let them in, and though they then tried to break through the door, he eventually heard them ride off.

If he'd stayed at home that night, his fate might well have been very different. For at 5:30 in the morning, when two servants arrived for work, they found all the doors locked, and couldn't raise either Jake or Betsy. They finally broke into the house and found a scene of bloody butchery. Jake (seventy-four) was dead, covered in blood, lying halfway off his bed, having been bludgeoned by some sort of heavy implement. Betsy (seventy-seven) was lying perfectly straight in her bed, battered with the same implement, five head wounds still bleeding. She lived on for a few days but never regained consciousness. A handful of silver coins was missing, and a couple of drawers had been rifled, but that was the only disturbance.

Two other servants were at first suspected, but convinced the authorities of their innocence. John (sixty-seven) offered a reward of five thousand dollars for any information concerning the murders, and even hired a private detective from Covington. What evidence there was seemed to lead to a bankrupt nephew, Adam Harper, who'd been bragging that he was about to come into a great deal of money (which he would have, after John, the last sibling, died), and he was publicly accused by a cousin, Wallace Harper.

The grand jury didn't indict him, however, and he slapped a half-million-dollar lawsuit on Wallace for slander—a sum that seems enormous in terms of the times—though from what I can tell the suit didn't succeed.

The murders were never solved and have been discussed and debated in the bluegrass for more than a hundred years.

I imagined the vicious mother and her daughter and son, as well as the silver in the cache in the wall that was carefully plastered over. The handgun is an accurate description of a very rare revolver I stumbled upon while doing unrelated research. I can't explain why I came up with any of that, but then that's the way writing is. I suspect I'm a romantic of sorts. Hidden staircases, secret panels, priest holes in old English estates—it all appeals to me.

The fact that the Harper murders seemed inexplicable and were perpetrated behind locked doors, murders that were never solved, helped draw me to them. And the rifts that were rent in the distantly related family—when the three elderly brothers and sisters had been the very best of friends—led me to consider inter-family rivalries that are sadly, most everywhere you look, a part of every-day life.

Edward Troye was a real-life Swiss-born Kentucky equine painter in the 1800s who had a very interesting life, and whose finely wrought paintings do indeed pro-vide almost all the visual information we have about the famous foundational Thoroughbreds from the 1800s. Asa Blanchard (1787-1838) was a much-respected silversmith too, whose work today (like Troye's as well) is extremely valuable.

I think the only real-life Thoroughbreds I mention by name are Lexington, Citation, and Bull Lea. I made up the names of all the other Thoroughbreds, and if by some strange coincidence I've come up with a name of a real horse, it definitely wasn't intentional. The horse farms—except for Claiborne, Calumet, and Spendthrift—are also entirely fictitious.

It's odd, when I think about it. I've watched only a handful of horse races in person. The sum total of my lifetime betting record is one single solitary dollar, because betting seems to me to be a highly irrational undertaking that holds no appeal. But I've stood by the rail at Keene-land at the crack of dawn, in all kinds of weather, to watch trainers breeze their Thoroughbreds as often as I've been to Woodford County, eating breakfast afterwards with the grooms and the hotwalkers, the exercise riders and the trainers and the owners, at the Track Kitchen.

I'm not Dick Francis. I can't write with his experience as a jockey or a trainer. I'm more in touch with the fringes of that world—the people who design and make the horse vans, the scientists who develop the treatments and medications, the veterinarians who work round the clock, often in tough conditions, the everyday folks who care for the horses, the down-to-earth owners who love them the way I do and ride for their own pleasure. I feel real concern for the racehorses too, who typically carry the burden—the ones who drive themselves because they care if they win, the others who can't, or wish they didn't have to try, and are shuffled from owner to owner till they meet some miserable end. I don't want to write about the racing game itself, with its sad, sad stories about bankrupt bettors, or the trainers and owners who can't pay their bills, or celebrity dabblers who fly in in private jets and make it look glamorous for an hour or two, while everyone else does the work.

ABOUT THE AUTHOR

Sally Wright is the Edgar Alan Poe Award nominated author of six Ben Reese mysteries, as well as *Breeding Ground* and *Behind The Bonehouse*, the first two Jo Grant horse country mysteries. Book 3 *The Outsiding* is published posthumously.

Wright's passion for telling the truth about things that mattered, such as horses, family business and human nature, led to the meticulous research for which she was noted. For her award-winning Ben Reese series she studied rare books, falconry, early explorers, painting restoration, WWII Tech-Teams, the Verona Code, and much more. Her hero Ben Reese, archivist-ex-WWII-Ranger, is based on a real person.

You can see more at http://sallywright.net/

www.ingramcontent.com/pod-product-compliance
Lightning Source LLC
Chambersburg PA
CBHW070900180626
46817CB00003B/850